I0659783

ANOTHER
Shot

A WILDCATTERS HOCKEY BOOK

BOOK 2

ALEXA PADGETT

Copyright © 2022 by Alexa Padgett

All rights reserved. No part of this book may be reproduced in any form or by any electronic or mechanical means, including information storage and retrieval systems, without written permission from the author, except for the use of brief quotations in a book review.

ISBN: 978-1-945090-41-7

This book is a work of fiction. All names, characters, locations, and incidents are products of the author's imagination. Any resemblance to actual persons, things living or dead, locales, or events is entirely coincidental.

Edited by Jessica Royer Ocken
Cover design by Chris Philpot

For Samantha.

Thank you for asking me to write hockey romances.
I've fallen in love with this team, and these men and women.
I hope you do, too.

CHAPTER 1
Cormac

I slammed my opponent into the boards, grinning behind my mouth guard as his helmet connected with the Plexiglas barrier with a resounding *thunk*. The whistle blared, and my shoulders tensed. Coach was already screaming, and for the first time in my career, the local fans booed me.

"Never talk about my wife again," I snarled.

Dukovsky gasped as he fell, his left pupil tiny, the right blown. *Good.* The fucker had a concussion.

"Ex-wife. She doesn't want you no more," he said in his thick accent.

I pulled off my gloves, intent on pummeling the rookie's face in—not just for these words, but for claiming he'd fucked Shannon. That she'd let him touch her.

Didn't matter that she'd served me papers, told me she couldn't be the wife I deserved or the mother to my children.

This twenty-year-old claimed my wife had taken him to her bed last week—to *our* bed, in the loft I owned. I swallowed bile as his next whispered words swirled through my head.

"Your ex-wife's pert ass has the cutest hockey tattoo. Good thing I play number twenty-two, too."

The only way he could know that was if he'd seen Shannon's

naked body. That small double-digit was so high on her left butt cheek that it wasn't visible even when she wore a swimsuit.

He'd been inside of her. As I stared down into his smug face, I knew it. And I also knew she'd done it to force me to sign the papers.

I barely heard the refs toss me from the game. I never caught my coach's angry words.

None of it mattered. Not now.

Shannon had told me she didn't want kids—never wanted them. I hadn't believed her, hadn't wanted to consider she'd keep something so essential from me. But she'd told me again when I suggested we try. She'd freaked out when she went off the pill, struggling to let me be intimate with her. When she started taking the birth control again, she cried tears of joy. She'd told me her position on children for the last time when she handed me the divorce papers.

I planned to sign the damn papers and give her what she wanted, because I'd always given Shannon what she wanted. She was the love of my life, and though it pained me to move out of our home, to un-link my life from hers, I'd assumed, naively, that she just needed some time.

But that wasn't it at all. Instead, she was telling me she'd left me behind. I should have realized that when she accepted the high-powered position at a Montreal law firm where she now worked ninety-hour weeks. Rarely did she return my calls, and she never showed interest in getting together when I was in town.

But she'd kept our—*my*—loft, and I'd stupidly thought that meant something.

Until Dukovsky opened his mouth and spewed shit all over my future.

Now I wondered if I'd ever known Shannon.

I sat in the locker room for the rest of the game, head bowed, not answering the staff's questions. I didn't even bother to raise my head when the rest of the team trailed in, quiet enough for me to know we'd lost. And I didn't hear Coach Gauthier bark my name.

My best friend, Pete, nudged my shoulder. Anger sat below the pity in his eyes. "Coach called you in."

I stood, my muscles groaning because I hadn't stretched. I met each teammate's gaze on my way toward Gauthier's office, giving them ample time to question me. Each one dropped his eyes. Felix, my other good friend and our goalie, clamped his jaw tight, just as angry as Pete was. The rest of the guys... They might hate me, too. I'd cost us a playoff game. They had every right to be angry.

I opened the door, my heart in my throat. Without Shannon, hockey was all I had left. But I'd fucked it up out there. Badly.

"You'll get a suspension," Gauthier said, his voice growly as he struggled to remain calm.

I hung my head.

"Which means we're without our best defensive lineman. For the rest of the fucking *finals*."

Inhaling through my nose, I remained silent. My hands fisted. Had I let Shannon take my career, too? Hockey paid for her to attend that fancy law school. My salary paid for the loft, her sweet little Mercedes. Oh, she'd liked the trappings of my life— just not enough to have my kids and tie herself to me forever.

That's what I thought we'd agreed to when we exchanged vows seven years ago.

I ignored the throb in my right fist. Dukovsky had deserved each punch.

"Nothing to say?" Gauthier made a disgusted sound. "I expected more out of you, Cormac."

He glared as I clenched my jaw. "I fucked up."

Gauthier leaned forward. "No kidding. That's why I'm considering the request that came in for you. You might be a dominant player, but you may well have cost those guys out there a championship. All because of one mouthy rookie."

I swallowed again.

"It's to the expansion team," Gauthier continued, his face reddening. "Before tonight, I never would have put your name on the list. Now you're a liability."

I dropped my gaze. Yeah, I was. And Dukovsky could end up with the Cup because I'd loved the wrong woman.

"All year you've been hot-tempered, unable to keep your head in the game." Gauthier shook his head. "That's not the player I signed on this team. And that's not a man I want here."

I nodded once, not lifting my gaze from my skates. This was worse than signing the damn papers. This was my career.

"Don't bother suiting up anymore. Soon as those boys finish the season, you're gone."

~

At least I could still play hockey. Sure, it was an expansion team in Houston, a city I knew nothing about, in a state I found miserably hot…

I settled on the bench back out in the locker room, still not bothering to remove my sweater or pads. I stared at my skates and waited for the rest of the guys to clean up. Once the locker room was empty, I removed my gear, my hand lingering on my sweater before I balled it into the laundry bin. I took a long shower, hoping the heat would release the ache of the lactic acid built up in my legs. No such luck. I dressed with methodical precision and exited the building with my head down.

My car was an older-model SUV I'd had for the last seven years. I'd never gotten myself something new; instead, I'd bought Shannon a car. As I approached, Pete leaned against the side of it, looking relaxed.

"Guess it didn't go well with Gauthier," he said.

"He's sending me to the expansion team."

Pete cursed. "Houston? What do they know about hockey?"

"Does it matter? I cost you guys the game, maybe the title."

Pete rested both hands on my shoulders. "You're good, Bouchard, but you're only one defenseman. We're a team. You don't have to shoulder this alone."

I glanced away, jaw tight. "Yeah. I do. I should have known better—"

"Than to love your wife? Hell, I still don't get it. Shan loves you, too. Everyone can see it. What happened?"

I met his gaze, and everything cracked open. "She doesn't love me enough to have a child with me. Her career, the one I paid for her to get, is more important to her. And she fucked Dukovsky to make sure I understood where I live on her list of priorities."

Pete's mouth dropped open. Then his gaze narrowed. "That's what Dukovsky said? He talked about your *wife*?"

I nodded once, unable to say more.

"That little sack of shit," he growled. "Did you tell Gauthier what he said?"

I shook my head.

"Not to Houston! We'll talk to him tomorrow, explain—"

I shook my head again, harder. "No. This is what I need. I let her own my head. I put her before everything. And look where that got me."

"Sent to freaking Texas! They don't understand what a puck is—"

"And that's my fault. I shouldn't have allowed Dukovsky to get to me."

Pete scoffed. "*Shannon* shouldn't have done you like that."

"But she did. And I have to live with letting you all down instead of stepping up like the veteran I'm supposed to be."

"So Houston's your punishment?"

"Appears so. And maybe…maybe a fresh start." I laid my hands on his shoulders. "I don't want to see her again, Pete."

He looked away. "Yeah, I get that. I see how much you love her."

"Loving her was a mistake." I moved around Pete and entered my car. "I'll tell the boys goodbye, if you think they'll let me."

Pete shook his head. "They're pretty angry about the loss."

"Yeah. Right. Well, for what it's worth, I'm sorry."

He met my gaze. "Me, too."

I slammed my door shut and started my car. I backed out of

the spot and drove toward my small apartment, the one I'd always known was temporary.

Apparently it was, but not for the reason I'd hoped. I wasn't moving back to my sun-filled loft with creaky hardwoods and a fabulous view of downtown. I was moving to Houston to finish my career on an expansion team that would be lucky to place above last.

My career was as dead as my marriage.

When I got home, I signed the divorce papers sitting on the kitchen counter, exhaustion blanketing me as I finished. Pulling my stuff out of my bag, I set my wallet and phone on the cardboard box I used as a nightstand.

My phone lit up as soon as I turned it on. I sneered at Shannon's name.

I'm so sorry about tonight, Mac.

She'd broken us and nearly broken me. I couldn't care less what she did now. I was done with her. Done with everything here.

I hit block and powered down my phone.

CHAPTER 2
Cormac
FIVE YEARS LATER

"I can't believe you gave Shannon tickets to your game," Pete said.

I shrugged. "She'll be in town for a conference. She loves hockey."

Over the years of seeing Shannon at my parents' place during my infrequent visits and her continued attempts to stay connected, I'd thawed my angry stance against my ex-wife. She and I had slowly settled into a comfortable, even close relationship.

The silence built for so long, I fidgeted, shifting my phone against my ear.

"You shouldn't be so friendly with your ex-wife," he finally said. "Especially one who got you banished to Siberia."

I snorted out a laugh. "Houston is opposite of Siberia—no snow, lots of people, culture…"

"You talk about the city as if you like it."

I looked out at The Galleria and Westheimer along the Houston skyline from the second-floor windows of my Rivercrest home. With four bedrooms total on the three-plus-acre estate, my house was modest compared to those of many of my team-mates who'd moved into the area. But I lived alone and didn't see that changing, ever. The house was much more than I needed, but it was close to the arena, many of the city's best restaurants, world-class medical facilities, and two airports. Houston's driving culture had taken some time to get used to, but now I couldn't imagine living in a loft in the heart of Montreal.

A small smile formed on my lips as I remembered my awe at the size of the place Shannon and I had chosen—and how it had cost more than my four-thousand-square-foot home here in Houston.

"I do like it," I replied. "And I'll take you to the Vietnamese place you loved so much when you visited last summer."

I'd rarely traveled home to Toronto since the divorce. My mother hadn't forgiven me for not working out my issues with Shannon and giving her grandbabies, and I was angry with my mother for pushing Shannon toward motherhood before she was ready—not that Shannon seemed ready even now.

"I love that place," Pete muttered. "How did your Hockey Siberia turn out to be such a good move?"

"Maybe because Coach Whittaker made me captain."

Pete grunted. "He sure whipped your band of misfits into shape."

I smiled. "Sure did."

"I didn't expect you to be in serious running for the Cup."

"Not this soon anyway."

"If things shake out as they look like they will, you'll play your old team for it."

"Don't jinx us. We have more than a quarter of the season left." I paused. "That said, I'll feel a little bad about you, but beating Gauthier and Dukovsky will be sweet."

Pete grunted. "I bet. Gauthier feels bad about the whole situation. You could have explained what happened—"

"He could have *asked*, too, instead of assuming the worst and bulldozing me. He undercut me to the team. I couldn't stay there after that interaction with my coach."

"In fairness, he listened to me when I told him why you beat the snot out of Dukovsky." Pete sighed. "Just a few months too late."

"After he'd signed the bastard," I said with a scowl. I hated the guy—that would never change. "He's still the greatest excrement pipe in the league."

Pete's chuckle drifted through the line. No one liked Dukovsky, not even his teammates, which now included Pete. That was the reason Pete had talked to Gauthier about my history with Dukovsky a few months after I was traded; Pete had wanted to keep the old goat from signing the problematic player. But Gauthier signed him anyway. Toronto had played well each year since, but they didn't have the chemistry we'd once had—before I smashed Dukovsky into the boards and left the city in disgrace.

"Top scorer, though," Pete noted.

"For now," I replied. We had an excellent young prospect here in Houston, still acclimating to the league, who looked more than capable of taking on Dukovsky. We'd also signed Jagger Naese during the offseason—a suggestion I'd made to Coach Whittaker after watching way too much footage in my media room. What else was I going to do?

Naese was a hardworking twenty-five-year-old who every other team had ignored, pushing him to the second or third line. Since his move to the Wildcatters, he'd led our first-line scoring and had the most assists in the league.

"Well, I'll see you next Sunday," Pete said as we finished our conversation.

"Looking forward to it."

He sighed. "Something tells me that's not because you'll be seeing my ugly mug."

I chuckled. "It's always good to see you, Petey."

"Still can't get used to being on the coaching side of the game."

He'd blown out his knee the year before, and Gauthier had made the right choice in moving Pete to be the offensive line coach. Unfortunately for Pete, that meant he spent more time with Dukovsky now. But Pete had made his choices, just as I'd made mine.

I clicked the phone off and continued to contemplate the skyline. Houston lacked the beauty of my home, thanks to its mishmash of zoning and swampy foundation, but its allure was outside the natural setting. The huge, writhing metropolis teemed with life and culture. I felt at home here—the loose cannon who'd found his place. Well, mostly.

I turned back toward my empty room and empty bed with a sigh. As much as I appreciated the space and beauty of my home, I hated that it remained unoccupied. The silence pressed against me, reminding me of my greatest dream: I still yearned for kids. But the likelihood shrank with each passing year, especially since the idea of dating, let alone getting married again, caused my chest to seize.

I'd considered adopting, but that wasn't a good option until I quit hockey. It sucked that I had to give up one dream for the other.

"Maybe I should get a dog," I announced to the empty space.

In a few months, I'd be thirty-two. I wanted to play for a few more years. However, to hedge my bets, I'd already talked to Coach Whittaker about taking on some more managerial tasks so I could learn the ins and outs of coaching. He'd been receptive to the idea, as long as my productivity on the ice remained high.

Since I had no family to come home to, I now focused on both. I hated that reality, but it *was* reality. And Houston was home. Now I just had to learn to enjoy living again.

My alarm blared, and I groaned, reaching for the small, black box of evil. Mornings weren't my thing. Getting up with the sun offended not just my mind, but all my muscles. Didn't matter, though, because practice was starting earlier than usual this morning to accommodate the open skate with a group of kids with special needs from the city's schools we'd have visiting us after, something Coach insisted on twice each regular season—once in December and once at the end of the season.

I'd asked him why in December, and he told me because his niece, Trixie, had confessed once that there was something magical about ice skating near Christmas. She'd moved in with him a few years back. Her sentiment had stuck with him, so he'd turned it into a Wildcatters' tradition.

This was one of the coolest parts about playing for Houston—the amount of outreach and community service we did here. We might have been a youthful team without a championship to our name, but the Wildcatters were well-loved, with most games sold out long in advance—not bad for an expansion team in a city with professional football, baseball, and basketball teams as well.

As soon as I remembered what day it was, I swung my legs out of bed, excitement sizzling up my spine. I adored working with these kids—their enthusiasm rubbed off, making me just as eager as they were to experience ice skating. I loved bringing smiles to their faces, loved seeing so many small people on our ice.

I dressed in a black T-shirt and my favorite jeans. Sliding on my sunglasses as I pulled out of my driveway, I still squinted against the rising sun. My new, old SUV that I'd bought when I moved to Houston withstood the hours of traffic I crawled through each week. A comfortable hybrid, the vehicle met my standards. I didn't need new and flashy like some guys. In fact, I'd found I liked the reliable, preferring to fix and clean up some things rather than buying shiny and new.

Sure, the guys teased me, but I reminded them I planned to live off my money long after I quit playing. Many of the players, especially the younger ones, refused to believe their million-plus salaries would dry up one day. But I'd faced that reality at twenty-six when I sat in Gauthier's office, holding my breath as he decided whether to trade me or kill my career. He'd thought he'd done the latter by sending me to Houston. But so far, I'd proved him wrong. And I intended to continue—by beating his star scorer on Sunday.

Gauthier had reached out after Pete explained the whole sordid tale. But it was too little, too late. The man had been *my* coach, not Dukovsky's. I would never forgive him for introducing Shannon to the little shit while we were at a party, nor for signing

him. Once I let him know that, my former coach never reached
out again.

The team skate had gone well this morning, each line running
their plays with precision and leaving me optimistic about our
chances for the second half of the season…as long as our guys
stayed healthy and focused. I never took the good times for
granted because I knew how quickly they could end.

Cruz and Nik skated in close, and I fist bumped them with
my gloves. "Great practice. You ready for this?" I grinned.

Cruz nodded, his expression his typical resting murder face.
The burly dude's facial hair bristled out from his jaw. He looked
scary as fuck in his skates and pads, which was ironic because he
cried at commercials and any movie with a dog in it. Cruz's tears
were as regular as my lawn sprinklers.

"Think the kids will scream when they see me?" he asked, his
gaze darting around.

"Just don't smile," Nik said.

"Shove it, Nik," I replied. "They'll love you, Cruz. You
know why?"

"They'll scream," Nik said, a gleam in his eye.

"They'll love you because they know your interest in them is
genuine."

Nik snorted. "Don't believe this guy—he doesn't have any
rug rats."

"Neither do you," I responded with a scowl.

Nik's gaze caught mine, and the teasing expression slid from
his face. He swallowed. "Um. Sorry, man."

"Maybe I should go shower…" Cruz skated away.

"Too late," I said as little voices rose into shouts. As much as Nik's comment stung, I couldn't help but grin as I skated toward the mob of youngsters. They were plowing toward the ice like a tsunami.

CHAPTER 3
Keelie

Before today, I'd never realized ice had a smell—something sharp that bit into my nose. I hung back, letting Mrs. Ruiz and my friend Lisa, a second-grade teacher the kids called Ms. Vaughn, sort the students into their groups. They were noisy, more excited than I'd seen them before. But then again, few people got to ice skate in a professional rink.

"What do you think, Andy?" I asked to the child next to me.

The small boy sucked two of his fingers as he raised his gaze to meet mine. The skates gave the kids a few extra inches of height, but Andy was small. He'd been born premature with infant alcohol syndrome. While he was as physically able as many of his classmates, he remained shy and slow to join new activities.

He pulled his fingers from his mouth. "It's big."

"Yes, it is. Now that we tied your skates, are you ready to hit the ice?"

Andy shook his head. His dark hair fluttered around his ears. My heart melted. This boy—so gentle and sweet—never deserved other kids making fun of him. Already he struggled to find his place, and he was only in first grade. Anger boiled in my chest, a weight sinking in my belly.

Kids like Andy were part of why I'd gone into physical therapy after getting my undergraduate degree in social work. I knew the system could only do so much to protect a child.

It hadn't been the system that hurt me; my parents did that long before I met a social worker or occupational therapist. My low-income school had been chosen as part of a pilot program that brought in occupational therapists, and Ms. Anaya had helped me get back into the "regular" classroom. Without her, I never would have considered going to college, let alone getting a graduate degree.

"Let's get on that ice," I said, my tone bright if brittle. I hated thinking about my past, so I avoided it.

Because *that* was a healthy coping mechanism.

"Don't leave me?" Andy whispered.

"Never," I promised, taking his small hand.

"I don't know how to skate." He frowned down at his tiny boots.

"Neither do I, but I hold hands well. I won't let you go."

He sighed, eyes longing but still torn, thanks to his fear. A few of the kids laughed as they whizzed past, holding on to the hockey sticks a big player with wild facial hair held as he skated backward.

Andy tugged me forward, eager to join the fun.

After making sure we had a big-enough gap between skaters, we stepped out onto the ice. Good thing I held Andy's hand because he immediately flailed. He made a small gasping groan and fell. But another hockey player skated up and bent in half to grasp Andy under the armpits.

"Find your balance," he said.

My entire body warmed. Holy hotness. The man's voice

washed over me, intoxicating—better than any margarita I'd ever imbibed. I swallowed my whimper and forced a smile to my lips. "Thank you…"

"Cormac," he replied. His gaze darted up to mine. His eyes were a rich brown, surrounded by bristly, dark lashes. *Beautiful.* "Cormac Bouchard."

"Thank you for catching me, Mr. Cormac Bouchard," Andy squeaked. "The other kids would make fun of me if I fell."

Cormac smiled, showing white teeth. I thought hockey players didn't have all their teeth—where had I heard that? Cormac's weren't braces-straight, but they were nice. I caught myself, shocked to be fan-girling over a man's *teeth*. I glanced up, met his eyes again. *Much* better than his teeth…

"You okay there, Andy? Ready for a trip around the ice?" I asked, yanking my mind from Mr. Hockey Player. No doubt he had a beautiful wife and athletic children at home.

"I'll take him," Cormac said, looking back up at me. "You don't have on skates, and it's harder to stay upright in tennis shoes than you'd expect."

I kept my attention on Andy. He was my responsibility today, the reason I was at the rink—*not* to lust after a hockey player.

"You okay with that, Andy?"

The boy chewed his lip, looking out at his laughing classmates. "Yeah, Ms. Keelie. I'm going to learn to skate now."

I smiled, and I thought I heard Cormac draw in a breath, but that made little sense. *Focus.* "You'll wow us all," I said, giving Andy's hand one last squeeze before I let go. My heart slammed against my ribs as I watched Cormac's sculpted backside flex in his uniform pants as he slid with such grace over the ice. The man seemed to have my libido on direct-dial, and I didn't like that.

I stepped off the ice and resisted the urge to fan my face. I settled into a comfortable spot to observe, but the longer I watched Cormac with Andy, the more my ovaries wanted to explode. The big man remained patient, even though Andy struggled. He let the other guys handle the more athletic kids while he helped Andy build confidence.

The hour ended, and most of the kids tromped off the ice. Andy glided around the rink with the agility some of the other kids had shown much earlier. When he made his third lap, his smile grew to huge proportions. I rested my hand over my heart,, the grin echoing my charge's.

"Thank you," I whispered to Cormac when they stepped off the ice.

"My pleasure. This kiddo's got drive. That's going to take him far." He offered Andy his fist, and again, those flutters pulsed through my tummy. Andy's fist met Cormac's much bigger one.

"Ah, Andy, you should have shared Bouchard with us," one kid grumbled.

Cormac chuckled. "I'm not as fun as Cruz the Cruiser. I saw him whipping you guys around."

The kids chattered again, louder thanks to their excitement after time with professional hockey players.

"Seriously," I said to Cormac. I met his eyes, the luscious brown melting into my soul. "Andy's a doll, but because he's slower, the other kids give him a hard time. And his mom works a lot, so he spends most of his days in the classroom with me."

Cormac's brows puckered. "I didn't know that was possible."

"Special needs classrooms are different. I work with a handful of kids, not an entire class. My students have more and more-complex needs."

Cormac nodded, running his free hand over his chin. "You care," he stated.

I laughed. "There's a saying: I love the work, not the pay." My cheeks burned. That probably wasn't appropriate. What if he thought I was commenting on his salary? Panic rose. "I didn't mean—"

"Time to go!" Ms. Vaughn clapped her hands. "Make sure you've collected everything."

I turned on my heel and hurried over to a group of four kids. Andy had removed his skates and swung his slip-on-shoe-clad feet as he sat on the metal bench. Next to him, his classmate Lori sat, tearful, hands fisted, unable to release the knot she'd made.

"Remember what we talked about?" I asked her.

"Yeth, Mith Hayth."

I plucked at the knot.

"I need to ath—ask for help."

"Right. Or you can take a deep, deep breath, fill your belly, and try again."

"The knot got all tangled." Lori scowled.

"And now it's out," I said. "Slip on your shoes, and I'll take back your skates."

Lori did as I directed while I collected the skates we'd borrowed. I marked each pair and placed them in the large tub, which I then hefted onto my hip.

We were most of the way through the stadium when I heard Cormac call, "Ms. Hayes!"

I stopped walking and set down the plastic bin, thankful for a respite. All those skates were heavy. Cormac puffed as he skidded to a halt—in his socks. He must have sprinted the whole way. My heart warmed.

"You left one." He waved a gray-and-blue skate, which looked tiny in his big hand. He still stood head and shoulders above me.

"Thank you." I nodded.

The group of students and teachers continued to move down the hall. "I enjoyed meeting you today, Ms. Hayes," he added.

I blushed as I opened the bin. "Keelie." At his questioning look, I said, "My name's Keelie. And it was a pleasure to meet you. Thank you again for spending time with Andy—"

"Have dinner with me."

I blinked up at him, noting his short, dark hair and his soft, pink lips, framed by days-old scruff. My tummy tumbled. "What?"

"Dinner. Let me take you out to eat."

"I…"

Cormac pressed a piece of paper into my hand. His fingers were warm and sent tingles up my arm, straight to my belly. "Andy said you like ramen. I can meet you at Jinya if you don't want me to pick you up. Tonight?"

CHAPTER 4
Cormac

"Ms. Hayes! We need to get these kids on the bus," one of the other teachers called.

Keelie flushed again, her cheeks the sweetest pink—a lovely contrast to her lightly-tanned skin. "Coming. Just getting the missing skate in here."

She'd pulled her light-brown hair back in a ponytail, and it reminded me of a thick stream of honey.

I hadn't dated a woman since high school. My moves were rusty—but not rusted. I gulped, shocked by how much it meant to me that she'd agreed. My heart thumped hard, and I curled my toes in my damp socks, hoping like hell my feet didn't stink. But I knew they had to because I'd been on the ice for hours.

Keelie dropped her lashes, covering her sky-blue eyes. She snapped the lid on the bulky plastic bin and bent her knees, widening her stance as she clutched the edges.

I bent to help, using my hand to guide the bottom upward and into her arms. Keelie was fit, her biceps flexing in her short-sleeved top, so I didn't offer to take the bin.

I'd learned with Shannon, though she preferred more intellectual pursuits, not to assume that a woman wanted or needed my help. Keelie was clearly capable.

She glanced at me, appreciation flashing across her expression.

"I'll see you there at seven thirty."

Her voice was warm but also a little throatier than the typical woman's, reminding me of sex. Hot, steamy, sweaty sex…which I hadn't had in far, far too long.

I clenched my fists, trying not to let those thoughts embarrass me, but I still had to shift because my pants were suddenly more constraining. As she turned away, she caught sight of my smile. She grinned back—bright and gorgeous—before she trotted after her group.

The back view was just as good as the front. She wasn't overly tall but she was well-rounded in all the right places. Her trim legs flared into her rounded ass before tucking back in at her waist. She strode forward, unfaltering, even though that bin weighed fifty or more pounds. Her ponytail swished between her shoulder blades like a clock pendulum.

Much as I wanted to fist pump, that felt like too much, so I just moseyed back to the locker room once she slid out of sight.

"You ran out in a hurry," Cruz said, dropping my skates on the bench next to my locker.

"Wanted to give the teacher the skate I found." I'd held it back when I found it on the ground under a bench so I'd have a moment to talk to her alone.

"That all you wanted?" Maxim asked. After so many years in the States, only hints of his Russian accent still inflected his words, and anyway, the man practically growled most of the time. But he was a good teammate and a better person. Maxim had never enjoyed my level of fame—or infamy, lucky him—because he wasn't showy. Instead, he maintained a stoic, even distant persona with the media and fans. I clapped him on the shoulder.

"No, it wasn't all I wanted. I'm taking Keelie to dinner tonight."

"Look at that," Nik said, sliding in next to me and elbowing my ribs. "Mac's got game."

Maxim nodded, his face still in neutral lines. "He's one of the best in the game."

"Not hockey, dipshit," Nik replied.

That got Maxim to smile enough to see his crooked lower front tooth, which made Nik grunt and Cruz guffaw.

I loved my teammates, but I shook my head as I strode toward the showers.

"Are you going to give us the play-by-play tomorrow?" Nik asked.

"Not in a million years," I replied.

"Aw, c'mon. You getting some action is five years in the making. You haven't been out with anyone since—"

"Shut up," Maxim hissed at Nik. I heard flesh hitting flesh and assumed Maxim had smacked him, but I didn't look back to find out. I'd refused to talk about my divorce or my lack of a love life. That was *my* business.

Just like Keelie was.

~

I don't know how to date. I'm going to be so damn bad at this. I popped another breath mint because why not? Then I fiddled with the door handle. Should I get out? We were meeting at 7:30, and it was still a few minutes until then. I fidgeted, unsure what to do.

I hadn't been so nervous…ever. Shannon and I had known each other since middle school, and I'd known she liked me before I asked her out. I hadn't been overly interested in the few women I'd taken out since my divorce, so I hadn't cared what they thought about me.

But I cared what Keelie Hayes thought. I wanted her to be as attracted to me as I was to her. I checked my hair. It looked like hair. I rubbed my still-smooth chin, thanks to the late-day shave.

I glanced over as a woman walked by—a woman in a pretty dress that showed off toned legs with tight calves that slid up under the soft hem of her skirt. Heat gripped my belly.

I shoved open my car door. "Keelie!"

She turned, her hand coming up to rest on her heart. "Oh, Cormac. You…you scared me."

"Sorry. I'm sorry." I patted my pockets, making sure I had my keys, wallet, and phone. I shut the door to my vehicle and locked it with the fob before striding toward her. "I've been sitting here, wondering if I should go up to the door, worried you wouldn't show—"

Her brows pinched. "I'd never stand you up."

I licked my lips, my heart rate kicking up. "Thanks." My tone was huskier than normal, and I know she didn't understand how important her words were to me. Shannon had treated me as a hockey player—practically indestructible, without feelings. I'd coddled her, wanting to protect her from the hurts of the world, but she'd never shown me the same consideration.

I hadn't realized that, or how much it hurt, until now. But maybe Pete was right. Maybe I'd returned to being friendly with

Shannon just because she was the only woman in my life.

But not anymore. I smiled at Keelie, who continued to peer up at me, tilting her head to the side. She wanted to figure me out, too. I was a puzzle, but I hoped by the end of our meal, I would be more than that.

"I almost called to cancel, though. I, ah, Googled you…"

My chest compressed as if someone slammed me into the boards. "You saw me acting out back when I played for Toronto."

She fidgeted before touching her hair, trailing her fingers upward and tucking it behind her ear. A small gold hoop snuggled against her lobe and three more tiny blue gems winked from holes farther up her ears. This woman enticed me—a contradiction of class and feisty Bohemian spirit.

I wanted to get to know all of her. "Can I tell you about that inside? Or would you feel more comfortable talking about it out here?"

Keelie snorted. "In a dark parking lot with a man twice my size?"

"When you put it that way…" I waved her forward. "Let's go in."

As much as I wanted to place my hand at the small of her back, to guide her, to touch her to see if her skin was as warm as I imagined it to be, even through the material of her dress, I didn't. Not with her so wary of me.

My *bad-boy phase*, Pete had called it. I grimaced, tugging at my collar. I didn't want to begin by explaining my failed relationship to Keelie, a woman I wanted to romance.

But she deserved to know.

Hell, part of me wanted to tell her everything—and to make sure she wanted kids. Because if her life goals aligned with mine and if our chemistry remained this hot without touching, I might never let Keelie go.

Though that made part of me want to run fast and far, because those feelings were almost entirely foreign. And after five years of feeling nothing, they were certainly too much, too fast.

CHAPTER 5
Keelie

By the time we were seated at a table toward the back of the restaurant, I'd chewed off my lip gloss. I'd assumed Cormac relished the attention and hero worship that came with his professional-athlete status, but so far, he seemed much more focused on me than on the other diners.

He slid my chair in for me before he rounded the table. I peeked at him again. The fine, dark-gray wool of his suit fit him well. He'd left two buttons of his dress shirt undone, showing off the tanned column of his throat. He undid the single button on his suit coat before settling into his chair.

He smiled at the waiter, who handed us menus, but there was tension around his mouth.

"We'll need a minute before we order." He glanced at me. "Is that okay?"

I nodded. Like Cormac, I wanted to get this awful tension over with as quickly as possible. He set his menu down in front of him and rested his forearms on it, clasping his hands together.

"They drafted me right out of high school," he began. "To the NHL, not the minor leagues. That first year proved a brutal lesson in the differences between junior- and professional-level competition." He paused, falling into some memory.

"I married Shannon, my high school sweetheart, before we

moved from our small town outside of Toronto into the city. She wanted to attend the University of Montreal in pre-law. Eventually she became a lawyer."

I knew all this…and I wasn't sure how it made me feel. I didn't love that he'd been married before, but really, what man in his thirties didn't have a past? I was twenty-six and had plenty of mistakes under my belt.

At my nod, he continued. "She started working at a law firm, but I wanted her to focus on our marriage—the family we'd postponed so she could finish school and start her career. She…didn't want those things."

I reached out and laid my hand over the top of his clenched fists. "I'm sorry."

"When she told me she never wanted a family, that her career was more important than me, that she wanted a divorce, I felt used. I'd paid for her education, and then she ditched me."

Wow. I hadn't read *that* on the internet. "Totally understandable."

"But I still loved her."

I sat back, removing my hand, feeling as if a boulder sat in my lap, crushing me. "Oh."

"That's when the write-ups about my bad temper hit the papers. I drank more—the reporters said I was partying more—but it was too many beers, trying to forget the hell I was living. Anything I did or didn't do, like missing a visit to the children's ward at the hospital, made the papers." He hung his head. "I just couldn't go. Seeing other people's kids, knowing my wife didn't want kids with me…"

Oh, this man. I blinked back tears and held my tongue.

"When I dragged my feet signing the divorce papers, she had an affair with another player. That led to the fight on the ice—the one that landed me in the penalty box during an important playoff game. My actions were stupid. I knew better."

"You were hurting," I murmured. "And since you came to Houston, the press has had only glowing things to report. I wondered about that—the change."

Cormac's expression set, his eyes earnest and filled with shadows. "Getting out of Canada ended up being an excellent move for me."

I took a deep breath. "My childhood wasn't easy—that's putting it mildly."

He shifted his jaw. "What does that mean? I'm fearing abuse…"

I shook my head. "No. More like…betrayal." I smiled, but it wobbled. "I'm being vague, I know, and I'm sorry. It's difficult for me to talk about."

"I understand," Cormac said. He rubbed a palm along the back of his neck. "Normally I wouldn't talk about my past either, but I'm attracted to you, so it seems important. What I'm feeling…is kind of freaking me out."

I blew out a breath. "Good. I've been freaking out, too!"

His lip curled up, not enough to call it a grin, but his intense expression softened. "I have to ask. I know it's forward, too soon—"

"Yes, I've always wanted kids," I said.

He sat back, dropping his hands into his lap. "How'd you know I was going to ask?"

I smiled. "I saw how you treated Andy today. And you said you were hurting too much to go to the children's ward because your ex-wife didn't want kids…" I emphasized the *ex*.

"All true." He smiled. "You're sharp."

I raised an eyebrow. "Or you're easy to read."

He tipped his head back and laughed. "No one's ever claimed that before. Well, maybe when I was in my angry phase."

I sobered. "I'm really sorry that happened to you," I said. No one should feel used or unwanted. Those emotions damaged self-confidence, further eroding trust and happiness. Unfortunately, I was all too familiar with that downward spiral, and I hated that he'd gone through it too.

"It was a long time ago," he said.

"You were so young."

He shrugged. "Now I'm not. I know what I want, and I'm going to get it."

I rested my chin on the back of my hand. "Oh? Do tell."

"Well, first, I want a glass of water."

I grinned. "I could use one of those, too."

"Then I want to eat something delicious while I get to know you better."

"Sounds good to me."

"And then, maybe at the end of the night…"

My heart pattered in my chest, trying to unmoor itself so it could float upward. "Yes?"

"I'd like to get your number so I can text you to make sure you got home okay."

I shook my head, laughing, some of the anxiety easing.

Cormac waved the waiter over, who brought us waters. I took a long sip.

"So…that's all you want?" I asked as I sat the glass down.

"Not even close. But those seem like achievable goals for tonight."

"Achievable goals." I chuckled.

He shrugged those heavy shoulders. "I'm an athlete. I think in goals—what I can manage, what I need to improve to hit the next level, next goal post."

I shot him a look from under my lashes. "I think you should aim higher."

CHAPTER 6
Cormac

The muscles in my chest, arms, abdomen, and thighs tightened as I took in her creamy complexion and long, dark lashes. Keelie applied her makeup with a light hand—her shadow was a neutral brown, her mascara darkening and probably lengthening her lashes. Her cheekbones shimmered a pale pink, while her lips were coated in a gloss that accentuated their natural color.

I enjoyed looking at her—at the dramatic curve of her chin to cheek to forehead. My gaze settled on her plump lips for a long moment, which made my heated muscles even hotter.

"Noted," I said, clearing my throat. I both craved and fought the intensity of emotion Keelie brought out in me. I wasn't used to caring this much. For the past many years, I'd remained numb...or at least disinterested. Hell, just yesterday I'd planned to live alone forever.

I still did. Nothing had really changed.

Everything had changed. Except...everything *might* have.

Once we'd ordered, I sat forward, elbows on the table. "How did you get into teaching?"

"The usual way," she said with a smile. "I like kids, and I wanted to do something worthwhile. But I'm not a teacher. I'm an occupational therapist."

I frowned. "Is that like a physical therapist?"

Keelie nodded. "Yes, but I focus more on the child's well-being than motor skills, though I do that some, too. My job is to help kids who are struggling with anything from brushing their teeth and hair to tying their shoes to holding their pencil."

"Ah. I think I understand." I wasn't sure I did. I'd never heard of a school occupational therapist, but I didn't want to tell her that—my lack of knowledge made me feel out of sorts, but also intrigued me.

"It's a relatively new field," Keelie added, tucking her hair behind her ear. "But we're useful, I swear. The kids I work with struggle to fit in with some of their peers. So, my job is to give them tasks—occupations—that help them reach the same milestones."

"And you work with all the kids in need?"

She nodded.

"I already know you're good at your job."

Her eyes danced even as a smile danced across her lips. "Thanks for saying that, but how could you?"

"I saw you with Andy, remember?"

"I wasn't supposed to be there today," she said. "I was filling in for another teacher who fell and broke her ankle the morning of the trip."

The waiter set my plate in front of me as I sat back. I considered the pretty brunette across the table. "I guess that means I have to be thankful for her fall, because I'm happy to be sitting across from you tonight, Keelie."

Her smile, shy but pleased, grew. "Me, too."

We talked about hockey as we ate—I explained the term

hat trick and that our jerseys were called sweaters. She listened with care, her attention fixed on me. I'd never spent time with someone so…present. Keelie engaged all her senses. If she did this with Andy, I understood why the kid adored her. In a world where most people were pulled toward their phones or the conversations and antics of those around them, Keelie gave me her undivided attention.

Shannon never did that. I shut down that voice, not wanting to compare the two. But now that I'd seen the difference—now that I better grasped just how disconnected Shannon had been from my interests?—I understood how easy it had been for her to end our marriage.

Shannon never made me her top priority, but *I could be with Keelie.* I tried to shut down that voice as well. We finished eating, and I noted she still had more than half her meal left.

"May I have a to-go box?" she asked the waiter.

He brought her one along with the bill. I pulled out my credit card even as I frowned. "Are you sure you ate enough?"

The waiter whisked the check away.

She glanced up as she filled the box. "I was nervous."

"About me?"

"About being on a date with you, yes. I mean, you're famous, and I'm…me." She crinkled her nose in the most adorable fashion. "You're different than I thought you'd be."

"I hope that's a good thing," I murmured. The waiter dropped off the check. I added a generous tip and signed my name just as a group of college students stopped at our table and asked to take a selfie.

"I'll take your photo," Keelie offered.

"Thanks!" a tiny girl with a bubblegum-pink pixie cut chirped. I smiled politely, annoyed at the interruption but putting on my best face for the fans—they were the reason I got to play the game. No reason to irritate them or give my reputation another hit.

As the group moved away, clearly excited, I held up a hand, stopping the pixie girl's retreat. "Would you mind taking a picture of us?"

She grinned. "Hell yeah, I will. And I'll like it on social when you post it and tell everyone I got to take the first picture of Cormac Bouchard with his girlfriend."

Keelie's eyes went wide at that, so after I handed the bubblegum girl my phone, I slid my arm around Keelie's waist— something I never did with fans—and gave her a gentle squeeze. "Breathe, Keelie. It's not that horrible a thought, is it?"

She looked up at me, a small smile on those plump lips. "I think anyone would be proud to claim you as their boyfriend."

"Luckily, there's only one lady I want." I tapped her gently on the nose and turned to face our photographer. She must have pressed the button because she handed me back my phone. "You two are so cute," she gushed. "Thanks for letting me document that."

"Um, sure," I said, pocketing my phone.

Keelie said goodbye in her soft, honey voice. Bubblegum girl waved and took off after her friends, all hands and elbows as she gestured back at us.

"What was that about?" Keelie tipped her head back.

"Not sure, but it looks like more fans are going to come up now. I better walk you to your car."

Keelie chewed her lip as she picked up her box. This time, I rested my hand on the middle of her back as I walked a step behind her out of the restaurant, my chest puffing with pride.

"Thank you for dinner," she said. She side-glanced at me.

"It was my pleasure." I'd never meant the words more. When she stopped at her Prius, I bent down, intending to brush my lips against her cheek...and get that next date.

She rested her hand against my chest, her expression serious. "I think I gave you the wrong impression earlier—about how far I wanted to go tonight. That girl...she got me thinking." Keelie blinked up at me, her cheeks bright red. "I'm not ready to rush into something, no matter how great it could be."

"That's okay," I said. Disappointment mingled with relief. "I haven't dated, even considered being serious about a woman in..." My words trailed off.

Shannon had told me she planned to attend the game this weekend and wanted to go out to dinner. That needed to be sorted because now I didn't want to see Shannon. She'd made her choice, and I needed to move on. The way I'd initially planned to. Maybe that would be with Keelie. That thought made my heart gallop.

"Oh. I understand." Keelie ducked away.

CHAPTER 7
Keelie

"No, that's the thing," Cormac said. "You don't. I…I'm attracted to you. I haven't felt this way in years. Maybe ever. Until now, I hadn't been able to see a future for myself, but then you walked into the arena, and I couldn't look away from you." He seemed both resigned and frustrated by the fact—like he wasn't sure what to do with the attraction between us.

Something eased its grip on my chest as pent-up tension seeped past my lips. "If it helps, I like you, too." My face flamed. *Way to go, Keelie. You sounded as young as your students.*

Cormac studied me for a heady moment before he tipped my chin up and brushed his lips against mine…once…twice…thrice. I sighed, my body humming with pleasure from the whisper-soft caress.

He pulled back, his expression filled with raw hunger. *For me.* This sexy, powerful man wanted me. My heart fluttered at the surrealness of it all.

"Your number?" he asked, his warm breath tickling my cheek.

I rattled it off, and he sent me a text—my phone vibrated in my purse.

"Text me when you get home?" he asked.

I nodded, too overcome to speak. My emotions bloomed brighter. This man's intensity mesmerized me. I wanted more—of him, of this feeling he evoked.

"You were the best part of my day, Keelie."

I settled into my car with as much grace as a sack of potatoes falling off a table. I struggled not to fan my heated cheeks. That man did things to me. My insides were molten, and my knees softer than jelly.

"Bye," I murmured. I shut my door and started the ignition. *Bye?* I rolled my eyes. Why hadn't I said something smart or sexy?

Because he overwhelms you, Keelie, my girl. All that sexiness is too much for you to handle. He was, but that didn't mean I wasn't game to try.

I *really* wanted to try.

Once I arrived home, I texted him, as I'd promised.

Home safe! Door's locked and just kicked off my shoes. You were the best part of my evening, by far. Now I'll dream about you.

I pressed send before I realized what I'd written. When I reread it, I squeaked, slamming my eyes shut. "You damn fool."

I'll dream about you, too, pretty girl. But I can't promise it'll all be sweet. Would you want to get together on Sunday?

I wiggled, happiness bursting through my skin.

I'd like that.

He never played disinterested or coy. I appreciated that—no, I *loved* that. I hated mind games. With my family history, there was no way I'd ever be comfortable around someone who manipulated or lied. Cormac meant what he said.

He was so solid, and not just his big, muscled body. His mind remained grounded, and he went after what he wanted with determination. I admired that. I admired *him*, not just his tight booty and broad shoulders, but *him*, the man he was inside the gorgeous, muscly package—though the exterior was damn superb.

I bounced up and down, squealing.

"Oh, right!" I grabbed my leftovers and put them in the fridge before bending down to pet Slippers, my gray-and-white cat. She meowed, her green eyes bright.

"Girl, you won't believe my evening…" I chattered to her while we sat on the couch, cuddled together. Soon, yawning, I headed toward bed, still giddy from my date.

Cormac Bouchard had proved to be an unexpected, but definitely welcome addition to my life. In fact, I looked forward to seeing him more than I should have. Because in my experience, nothing good lasted—not a loving mother or a safe home or a faithful partner. But for now, I'd savor the giddiness pumping through my bloodstream.

CHAPTER 8
Cormac

I hit practice on Thursday morning still riding the high from my date. I was happy. Keelie Hayes might well be the best damn thing to happen to me.

"Guess the date went well?" Maxim asked after we'd showered and changed. We were heading out to a late lunch before we watched game tape for the game tomorrow.

"It did." I settled on the bench in front of my locker to tie my sneakers.

The guys all *ooh*ed.

"It was just a date," I said, but I continued to smile.

"You want to see her again?" Stol asked. He threw stuff into his gym bag.

"Yes." *No question there.*

"Are you going to make your relationship status social legit and post something?" Nik asked. He glanced over from his locker where he was putting on deodorant.

I shrugged. "We've been out once."

"But you're texting with her," Maxim said. "Right?"

I nodded.

"And you have plans to see her again," Stol added.

Again, I nodded. Maybe I should post our pic on social media. Bubblegum girl would expect the image to show up there. Was it too soon? If I posted about Keelie and me, would fans eventually expect a marriage proposal? That sobered me and caused my belly to jitter with anxiety. I'd just met the woman, and I liked her, but pushing for more...

Was I ready for that? Did I want to try commitment again? What if we crashed and burned?

She wants kids. My mind conjured an image of Keelie's body rounded with our child. Contentment settled over me as the image shifted to a blanket-wrapped infant and a little boy with my brown hair and her blue eyes. He'd be adorable.

I wanted that—at least in this moment—so I texted Keelie to let her know I was thinking about her.

The dots appeared, and my belly jittered.

And now I'm thinking about you! Looking forward to Sunday.

I grinned. Yeah, I definitely wanted to date Keelie.

The guys and I went to lunch and then to my house to watch the game footage in my media room.

"Why does Dukovsky have to have such a beautiful slap shot?" Maxim muttered.

We watched the asshole take another shot—and score. "Probably to annoy you," I said.

Cruz flopped back in his chair. The room had stadium seating and plush leather seats. I'd splurged on this room because I knew, as captain of the team, I'd have the guys over to watch tapes. We'd made it a weekly thing during the season. This was in addition to Coach's tape-time, so not all the guys were here—mostly the veteran players.

Maxim shook his head. "It annoys me. A lot. I want to shut that piece of shit down."

We discussed possibilities for a while before we worked out in my gym. By the time the guys left after dinner, it was too late to text Keelie again.

I shot off a quick hello the next morning before practice but had little chance to chat because I ended up busy with interviews that evening, thanks to a nasty scuffle during the game between Naese and another player.

By the time I finished responding to the media and showering, it was too late to contact Keelie again. "Damn, this place is big and lonely," I muttered as I walked into my house half an hour later.

Once I'd changed and climbed into bed, smashing my pillows in place to get comfortable, I brought up my photo app. I scrolled back through the images, searching for the best one of Keelie and me. There were a lot. And the way I looked at Keelie…the way she stared up into my eyes… We looked entranced by each other. Definitely infatuated.

I posted my favorite image with a heart emoji.

Then my muscles tightened, and this time not with desire. Screw all those thoughts about a kid. I wasn't ready for *that*—I refused to get left again. Last time, Shannon ripped my heart from my chest, and left me bleeding so badly that I nearly destroyed my career.

And that train of thought reminded me that I still needed to talk to Shannon and tell her I didn't think we should get together while she was in town. I'd postponed doing so, and I wasn't sure why. I just…didn't want to talk to her. Or see her.

I wanted to focus on Keelie—on how she made me feel.

But fuck. Getting serious about another woman? This indecision pissed me off. I usually made goals and completed all the steps to achieve them. That's what I'd thought I was going to do here.

I tossed my phone onto my nightstand and dropped my chin to my chest. My attraction to Keelie—*not* a strong-enough word—didn't mean I wanted to do more than date her. Or that I ever would…except I'd asked her if she wanted kids, and that meant I saw a future with her, didn't it? Possibly. Or not. Probably not. But Keelie wanted a family, too.

Shit. Everything had gotten way too complicated.

I woke Saturday and decided not to see Shannon while she was here for the game. I called and left her a message.

Next I called Keelie, but I got her voicemail. Unsure what to say, I didn't leave a message.

Antsy, I paced my living room, and I grabbed my phone when it rang. Maxim.

"Hey, man, what's up?

"Dukovsky's hurt."

"What—how?"

Dukovsky hurt? My fists clenched. No, I didn't want that. I wanted to be the one to crush the spineless runt, to embarrass him—to make him pay for mocking me and forcing me to realize my marriage was truly over.

"Practice. Something's wrong with his leg."

I gritted my teeth. "Thanks for letting me know."

"Yeah, man. This may be great news for us."

Professionally, absolutely. But I still wanted to pummel him, best him on the ice.

Keelie called me back as I hung up with Maxim, but I declined it as I suddenly wasn't in the mood to talk. Yes, I wanted to move forward with my life, but the Dukovsky news had caused all the rage and betrayal of my past to storm back to the forefront of my mind.

Instead of talking to the woman who'd lately dominated my dreams, I turned on the sports network and listened to chatter.

CHAPTER 9
Keelie

"He didn't call you? Text? Nothing?" my friend Marian asked, her voice holding an odd note. Her lips tugged down.

Okay, so maybe she wasn't as *gleeful* as she'd just sounded after I told her Cormac hadn't called me back to complete our plans. I steeled myself against the disappointment as I shook my head. "Not since yesterday, and then he didn't leave a message. Or answer when I called him back. But that's okay. We had fun." I pasted a smile on my face, though I don't think it convinced either of us of my blasé acceptance of Cormac's ghosting.

Slippers jumped onto the couch and curled in next to me, whiskers twitching. *Dammit.* My cat had intuited my despondency. My response to Cormac's rejection was ridiculous. I barely knew the man. I stroked Slippers' soft fur as my heart continued to ache.

Marian's phone pinged, and she picked it up, her eyes narrowing as her expression turned stony. "Guess this is why." She turned her phone toward me, showing me a picture of Cormac, his hand on the spine of a sleek and gorgeous blonde as they exited the arena.

That was *exactly* the type of woman I would have chosen for him. Marian's lips twitched. Her mood seemed off—but maybe that was me. "Weird that he posted that photo of you on the socials and then was seen with another woman just a couple of days later. I guess you're not his type."

My lower lip wobbled, but I slammed my mouth closed and gave one stiff nod. "Guess not. How did you find the photo?"

"I put the alert thing-y on my phone." She curled her lip.

"Why are you happy about this?" I slouched back on my couch and stared up at the ceiling. Its white speckles caught dust and looked like moldy cottage cheese. I wanted to change it, and was pretty sure I could, but DIY stuff scared me.

She shrugged. "I'm not happy. I just couldn't figure out why he'd want to be with you."

I flinched, my eyes going wide. Was she always like this? "Well, clearly, he doesn't." I hated that ceiling. At the moment, it reminded me of my life: a gross, hot mess. *This* was why I didn't do relationships. *Men weren't trustworthy.*

My mother's words echoed through my mind. Dammit, I didn't want her to be right about Cormac. I'd wanted him to be *special.*

I knew better.

"You're looking at it again," Marian said.

"It's right there." I gestured toward the ugly ceiling.

"Yes, but you won't do anything about it, so stop hating on it."

I lifted my hand from my cat's warm fur. "I could—"

"You won't." Her tone brooked no argument. "Look, it's okay to be a perfectionist who won't try anything new because you're not good at it yet."

My hands clenched at my sides, but I took it as a win that I didn't cross my arms as I pouted. This was the problem with having a long-time friend. She knew my weak spots…and she'd been pressing on them recently. I wasn't sure what the problem was between us, but she'd seemed angry since I told her about my date with Cormac.

"Stop trying to rile me up so I forget about Cormac." I dragged my hands over my face. "I liked him. He kissed me. It was a beautiful moment, but that's all girls like me get."

Marian shoved my thigh with her big toe. Her decorated toenail, with its tiny rhinestone flower on a soft red background, dug into my bare skin an inch below the edge of my sweat shorts. No reason to dress well if I was just moping around my place today. Sunday—the day Cormac had suggested for us to get together.

"Ouch!"

"Stop whining. It's annoying—and beneath you. You moved up from the wrong side of the city. Sure, you have a heap of student loans, but you also have a good job that might become a great job if you'd go into private-sector work."

I frowned, hating how she harped on this issue. "Working with kids was always my goal."

"And it's noble, if ridiculous, for your long-term plan."

"I can eat and have a car to drive. I'm fine. Plus, I get smiles and hugs every day. Who else can say that about their job?"

"Every other nearly-homeless teacher working two jobs to afford their shitty place in the world."

"Stop it. I love what I do. I adore my students."

Marian sighed as she shifted to rest her head on my shoulder. "Fine. This guy's messing with your feelings. That's uncool. And the school's not paying you a ton, and you have a nasty popcorn ceiling."

I rested my head on top of hers. "I'm going to make you scrape that ceiling with me one of these days."

Marian popped up off the couch so quickly that I yelped. "I brought supplies! And I know you've watched at least fifty hours on YouTube about how to do this correctly."

I pulled my butt off the couch, frowning. "That is what you want to do with your Sunday?"

She scoffed. "No. I'm not getting dirty. But this will keep your mind off the sexy-hot hockey asshole and improve your house's value all at once. Plus, then I don't have to look at the hideous ceiling anymore."

I accepted the scraper tool she handed me. "I'm not sure."

"Fifty hours of YouTube, Keelie. You're sure. Now, where's your ladder?"

A few hours later, I was alone with my sander. Marian had gone, but I finished the project—even though my arms were tired, and my shoulders ached from being over my head.

Finally, covered in grime but smiling, I felt satisfied with the effort. I placed my hands on my hips and smiled at my newly-smoothed ceiling. "Much better." Too bad this home improvement had come at the expense of my pride, but hey—that was a small price to pay. Cormac and I'd had a nice date. I'd misunderstood the connection, but I had a fun story to share at cocktail parties.

After washing my hands, I picked up my phone and noted a voicemail from a number I didn't recognize. I pressed play. "You leave Cormac alone," a woman growled into my ear.

I pulled the phone away, shock bouncing through my system. I wasn't sure what to make of that at all, but at the moment, I was too tired to even try.

I took a long, hot shower and fell onto my bed, asleep basically before my head touched the pillow—and before I'd set my alarm.

That's how I ended up running late the next morning. Nearly twenty minutes behind schedule, I never looked at my phone, just grabbed it from the charger and stuffed it in my bag.

CHAPTER 10
Cormac

As I sat in my car, staring at the long, low-slung elementary school where Keelie worked, I ran my fingers through my too-long hair. Nerves sizzled through my midsection, causing me to grunt in annoyance and pain. I hugged my ribs, thankful they were just bruised, not cracked as I'd worried after they took the brunt of the impact when the 270-pound D-man for the Flyers rammed into me. I was also thankful this impact had occurred a half-second after I'd flipped the pass to Nik for our one-nil win.

Frustration was the next emotion to wash over me because I'd missed out on seeing Keelie and instead spent Sunday evening at home, pacing my house, worried that she wouldn't forgive me for standing her up—even though I hadn't. At least I hadn't meant to.

On top of my concerns about Keelie, seeing Shannon after the game had sealed it for me: she was my ex for a reason, the woman of my past. That's why I was here now. Unfortunately, Shannon now seemed interested in spending more time together. That bomb had led to a deeply awkward conversation outside the locker room. I closed my eyes as I groaned.

"What's wrong?" Maxim asked.

"Keelie's never going to believe what happened. I wouldn't believe it if I hadn't experienced it firsthand."

"But it's the truth," Maxim said.

"So I should just go in there and say, 'After ignoring your call on Saturday morning, I met up with my ex-wife, who suddenly wants to get back together, probably because she saw the picture of us I posted. Oh, and the reason I didn't let you know about all that was because my good friend tossed my phone in Cruz's ice bath after our Saturday-evening skate.'"

I thought we'd wait to show until the end of the school day, but as soon as we exited the car and walked toward the school building, a ring of kids formed around us, and it continued to grow. I shuffled closer to the front steps as the group morphed around me.

"It's Cormac Bouchard!" a boy yelled.

Great. I hadn't considered being recognized and mobbed by a posse of schoolchildren.

"I'm here to see Ms. Hayes," I said.

"What for?" a girl asked. She didn't even come to my waist.

"I need to talk to her," I said.

"You got a problem?" another child asked.

I nodded. "And she's the only person who can fix it."

"In the entire world?"

I turned toward that voice and recognized the tiny boy I'd helped around the ice the other day. His lisp was adorable. So were his freckles. *Andy.* That was his name.

"Andy! Great to see you, my man."

Delight flashed over his face as I fist-bumped him. "It's good to see you, Cormac."

"Do you know where Ms. Hayes' room is?"

"This way." Andy slipped between a few of the bigger kids,

who deflated as they realized we weren't here to sign autographs or dote on them. Maybe another time. Definitely another time if this conversation with Keelie went the way I hoped it would.

"Here it is," Andy said, beaming. Then he shifted on his short legs. "I gotta go. My mom's going to worry because I'm not outside with my aide."

"Thanks for the help, kiddo," I said. "I'll get you some tickets to a game, if you want to come."

Andy's face lit up so brightly, I squinted. "Yeah! That would be fun."

I nodded. "Cool. I'll talk to Ms. Hayes about getting those to you."

Andy whooped as he ran down the hall, his backpack bouncing up and down.

"He's cute," Maxim said.

"He is. Now, help me fix what you broke so I don't need to use the cute kid to crawl back into Keelie's good graces."

"I didn't know it was such a big deal. We were just horsing around." Maxim turned petulant, but he raised his hand and knocked. Keelie's was the only closed door. Weird.

She opened it only a crack, peering out through the slit. Her eyes widened when she saw me, then grew further when she noticed Maxim. "What's going on?"

"We need to talk to you," I said. "Well, Maxim is here to tell you what happened. I'm here because…because I missed you."

Keelie remained nonplussed. "I'm meeting with a parent. Give me a few minutes."

She shut the door.

"She didn't seem happy to see you," Maxim noted.

"Why would she be? She thinks I stood her up. If she checked the stupid internet, she might even think I blew her off to spend time with Shannon instead."

Maxim rubbed his index finger over his lip. "I'm not sure I'm going to be enough help on this one, dude. I mean, she's giving you the cold shoulder. You, Cormac Bouchard."

I crossed my arms over my chest, agitation swirling through me. "I'm aware of my name."

"But are you aware that you're a catch? Chicks fall over themselves to get near you, and the one you want isn't interested."

"I don't want a random chick." I wanted Keelie. For a woman I planned to date causally, I missed her more than I should. She was all I thought about, even while I was watching the news coverage of Dukovsky's injury. I'd blown past casual in about seven seconds, but I clung to the idea that we'd hang out, even as worry about her not wanting to see me ripped at my guts.

I was a disaster, and I hated it.

While we waited, teachers streamed out into the hallway behind many of the kids lingering there. The crowd swelled, and I gritted my teeth as I forced smiles for the multitude of selfies that finally made my head ache. Maxim's temperament slid as well, and I worried he'd turn into a wounded bear. The only one worse than him in these situations was Cruz.

Then finally the office door opened, and a middle-aged woman slipped out with Keelie behind her. Keelie held open her door, her face a mask of disapproval.

"It's my fault Cormac didn't contact you yesterday," Maxim

began, tripping over his own feet to get into Keelie's room. "I pranked him, and his phone ended up in Cruz's ice bath, fritzed to hell... Please give me a minute away from all the flashes. My eyes..."

I slipped through the space just before Maxim slammed the door and leaned back against it, his chest heaving.

"That's worse than the mobs at the bars after a game," I said. "They're shorter and rowdier."

"I almost stepped on a kid," Maxim groaned, running his hands down his cheeks, expression filled with horror. "Like, a baby one."

"A kindergartener?" I asked. I hadn't seen any child that young outside.

"I don't know! It came up to my knee. And it squeaked."

My shoulders shook at his dramatics, but I managed not to laugh. He shot me a wink that I'm pretty sure Keelie caught. I straightened, blinking to rid my vision of the black spots floating there.

"What..." Keelie's brows tugged low, darkening her eyes. "Marian said you were out with another woman. I saw the picture."

"Shannon, my ex." I sighed. "And that wasn't really by choice. She came into town for the weekend—some kind of legal convention. I'd told her we shouldn't meet up, but she decided otherwise."

"Cormac escorted her to her car after the game," Maxim cut in. "He didn't go anywhere with her because he was too busy yelling at me about the damn phone. I bought him a new one this morning—"

"After rolling your lazy butt out of bed at eleven—"

"Because we didn't have practice today. And I'll point out that I came here to be blinded and deafened by the kids. Christ, they're loud." Maxim stuck his finger in his ear and winced.

"You can go," I said, leveling him a look.

He smirked, eyes brightening for the first time since I told him how he'd screwed me over. "No, I can't. You made me ride with you. Now you have to give me a ride home."

My jaw ticked. "Call a ride share."

"You really threw his phone in someone's ice bath?" Keelie asked.

Maxim nodded. "Yeah. See, Nik said that—"

"And you think that was an appropriate choice?" Keelie continued. "What if he'd had a family emergency? What if, say, your father had a heart attack, but you didn't know about it because your family couldn't get in touch with you? Would you think the prank was funny, then?"

Maxim wilted, swallowing hard, gaze shifting. "No, that wouldn't be funny."

"But you thought because no one was injured, it was okay. Just my feelings were crushed." Keelie settled her hands on her hips. She'd just used her teacher voice on Maxim, and that warmed my lower belly nearly as much as her words. Not that I wanted her feelings *crushed*—I didn't. But knowing she was into me caused my heart to swell.

Maxim shot me a desperate look, but my attention turned to the woman in front of us.

"And you…" She rounded on me. "There's the cloud. You

could have messaged me on your computer or something. If you really wanted to get in touch. Maybe that's the point—you didn't." Hurt and anger clouded her expression.

My lungs seized as if I'd just skated thirty laps. "I could? That's possible?"

"Yes, but you let me think you stood me up. I told you I wouldn't do that, so you turn around and do exactly that to me?"

My neck and face burned. Keelie, in teacher mode, was scary. "I... I didn't know—" I stuttered.

"I DIYed," Keelie exclaimed, "an entire ceiling." She glowered at both of us. "Do you know how messy that is? I probably still have stuff in my hair, and my shoulders have been killing me all day. For what? A silly game."

"Keelie?"

I snagged her hand, studying the soft, small appendage. Her fingers were long, tapered, beautiful. "I'm really sorry. We both feel terrible about it."

Keelie grunted, but she didn't pull her hand away. "You brought personal business here, to my school. My colleagues and the kids are going to think we're dating." Her cheeks grew pinker, but she lifted her chin, daring me to respond.

"Good."

"Good?" She blinked rapidly. "Why is that *good*?"

"Because that's what I want." I stepped in closer. "I was upset when I couldn't reach you. Like, really."

"He was," Maxim said. "Ow!" He glared and rubbed his ribs where I'd elbowed him.

"I told you before that I wanted to date you, to romance you.

Nothing's changed." Well, a lot had. I'd had a freak-out, but then when my phone—my only link to Keelie—was gone, I'd understood what I truly wanted: *her*. To date. For now.

She opened her mouth, but then slammed it shut. Her features softened and a look closer to adulation slid over her face. It caused my heart to race.

"Are you…serious?" she asked. Her tone turned soft, almost shy.

"Yes. I posted a picture of us together to social media." I showed it to her on my phone.

"Oh."

"That's all you have to say?" I asked. "A minute ago, you were full of righteous indignation."

"But…" Keelie glanced between Maxim and me. "But…you weren't supposed to want me. Marian said… I'm just…"

"Hot as fuck with that authoritarian vibe and three-button cardigan?" Maxim offered.

Keelie blushed again, and her expression wavered. "I'm sorry. I was mad and defensive."

"Don't be," I said. "I would have been if the situation was reversed."

"But I kind of accused you…" She dropped her face into her hands. "I feel terrible."

"Does this mean you forgive me?" I wrapped my fingers around her wrists and gently pulled her arms away from her face.

She swallowed, eyes wide, searching mine. I remained still, quiet. "Y-yes," she breathed.

"Great," Maxim said. He clapped me on the shoulder. "Now,

you owe me a beer and a meal. And I'm never coming to a school again."

"You're leading the Say No to Drugs program next month," I reminded him.

Maxim stomped toward the door, cursing a blue streak under his breath.

Keelie tucked her hair behind her ear, suddenly shy. "I really am sorry."

"You have nothing to apologize for."

"I might have wished bad things to happen to you."

I leaned down, brushing my nose along her cheek. "Would you consider un-wishing them now?"

She blinked those big, beautiful eyes at me. "Yeah."

CHAPTER 11
Keelie

As I walked out of the school with two huge professional athletes, Cormac dug in his pocket and tossed his keys to Maxim. "I'll get it from you later."

He nodded. "Sure. Nice meeting you, Keelie. I expect you to cheer loudest for me when you come to a game."

I smiled, but the skin felt stretched, as if my face wasn't sure how to handle this change of events. "Nice to meet you, too."

"Mind if I catch a ride with you?" Cormac asked.

"Well, no, since you just gave away your car."

"You seem nervous."

I licked my lips. "I am. I mean, twenty minutes ago, I wasn't connected to a celebrity."

He sighed. "Yeah, you were. You have been since the moment people saw us at dinner the other night."

Nerves fluttered in my belly. "I didn't know that, though."

Cormac stopped walking, so I did, too. We stood between two cars as he turned me to face him, his palms cupping my elbows. "I'm just me. Just like you're you. Get me?"

I nodded.

"I want to see where this attraction between us goes. Do you want that?"

"I do. I just… I don't know how to be involved with a

famous person."

He wrapped his arms around me. They were thick and warm, and I laid my cheek against the wall of his chest and closed my eyes, letting the experience calm me.

"If it makes you feel any better, neither do I."

I straightened up, and he loosened his hold but didn't drop his arms—as if he really wanted to be here with me. In a parking lot.

"I'd like you to come to my place," he said.

I gnawed on my lower lip as I looked up at him. His eyes burned with desire. I cleared my throat. "Sure. You'll just have to give me directions."

He smiled. "Then you'll know how to get there on your own. For next time."

Forty-five minutes later, we pulled into his driveway behind an ornate, black cast-iron gate. The house, a two-story made of red brick with white stone across the first-story façade, was an impressive presence. The door was a gleaming black, not unlike the colonial homes I'd seen on my trip to Philadelphia last year. My palms were sweaty as I took them from the steering wheel. Once again, the distance between Cormac's life and mine slammed into my reality.

I followed him up the steps, admiring the Travertine-tile flooring in the double-story entry and the gleaming wood staircase that swept up into an elegant arc, bisecting the space. Cormac walked toward the great room, which was indeed great. A TV nearly the size of a movie screen took up an entire wall. The three full-length sofas arranged in the space were sleekly modern, but not leather, as I'd expected. They were a rich brown tweed. The coffee table seemed to be a large drum.

Cormac saw me staring at it. "I got that on a trip through the southwest a couple of years ago. The top's cowhide."

I nodded, feeling dazed.

"Want a drink?" he asked.

"Sure. Water. I have some work to do later."

Cormac strode into the kitchen. The enormous range—a fancy one with a French name—dominated the space. His refrigerator was twice the size of mine, and he had those dishwasher drawers. Everything about the house screamed wealth and status.

"I'm the first person in my family to go to college," I blurted.

"I never even applied," Cormac responded as he opened the fridge. "You okay with filtered water? I try not to use plastic bottles since I saw that video online about sea turtles and plastic."

"Yes, of course." No doubt his water filter was fancy, too, but I'd grown up on tap water, so I wasn't picky. "I just meant our worlds aren't the same. I'm a school occupational therapist."

"Which I had to look up, by the way. I didn't even know that was a job until I met you."

"And I have a tiny house, just two bedrooms and one bath."

He handed me a glass before he poured another. "That seems big enough for one person."

I gulped the water, trying to get him to see my point. "You're rich, and I'm not."

He shrugged. "Money's not all that—and I know many people would disagree with me, but I'm serious, Keelie. I have a big house, and it's empty. I have the money to buy nice things, but I have no one to buy those things for. I rarely see my parents, and I don't have any siblings. I travel too much to have a pet."

I set the glass on the green-and-black-swirled granite bar where I'd stopped—right at the edge of the kitchen. "That sounds lonely."

"It is." He set his glass next to mine as he came to stand next to me. "I know parts of my world are weird, probably even scary."

"Very scary," I muttered. "I don't own fancy dresses or know how to do those cat-eye makeup tricks I see on celebrities. I wear comfortable clothes that kids spill on, nothing like your ex." I slammed my lips shut, willing the blush not to blaze across my cheeks.

It did anyway.

Cormac cupped my face. His fingers were warm, his palm large enough to cover the whole side. I closed my eyes, enjoying the feeling. From the first moment we'd touched, something had sparked between us. That wouldn't change—but that didn't mean I should pursue more between us either, though I wanted to. Desperately.

"I'm not used to getting what I want." I opened my eyes.

"Ah. You work hard, then harder, to get the results." He nodded. "That's what I've done every day since I was eleven and set my sights on the NHL. Hard work and perseverance— that's what got me here. As for Shannon, I can tell you she's in the past." He pursed his lips. "Actually, I can also tell you that comparisonitis often ends poorly, with me, at least, feeling like I didn't live up to some expectation. I don't like it. Instead, I do my best to meet, and preferably surpass, my previous attempts."

I leaned farther into his hand, wishing he'd touch me more.

"You seem to have all the answers."

He shook his head. "Not true. I've had some experiences, and I learned from them. Hopefully, I grew…eventually. But that doesn't mean I didn't flail my way through or wish them away."

I inhaled, drawing on my courage. "I'm worried you'll realize you could do better, and your rejection will crush me."

Finally, he stepped in close enough for our body heat to mingle. I lifted my hands and rested my palms on his chest, my fingers curling into the softness of his T-shirt.

"Do you know how many women I've dated since Shannon and I separated?"

I mashed my lips together, hating how much I wanted to know.

"None. I took a few nice ladies out for dinner, but there was only one woman I dated—we went on four, maybe five dates."

I searched his face. Cormac's open expression called to me. Truth gleamed from his eyes. "And if I'm honest, it was because I missed having a physical connection with someone. Or at least I thought I did. There wasn't any…I guess emotionality. Just a rather lackluster release…" He cleared his throat, seeming to realize I wasn't interested in that much detail. "So, I ended up hating the total experience, and I haven't asked another woman out since. Until you."

"Dating can be really hard," I said. Then I rolled my eyes at myself—what an inane reply.

His lips quirked. "Understatement of the year. But that's because it's challenging to find someone we connect with, right?"

I nodded. "I knew I wanted to get to know you, right from

the beginning." Again, my face flamed.

"Because I was famous?" he asked.

I shook my head, though I could understand his reason for asking. "No. I mean, I knew you were a hockey player, clearly, but I've only ever seen a game when it's on at a restaurant or something. I'm not a huge sports fan." Realizing I'd dug myself a hole, I hurried on to say, "That's because I don't understand all the rules in hockey. I know it's very athletic, doing what you do on narrow blades, and that you work out a lot..."

His eyes twinkled. "Keep talking. I like this whole direction of conversation."

I giggled. "I knew who you were—how good you are at hockey. But that had nothing to do with my interest in you. You were so kind to Andy, so patient, and *that* man, he's the one I wanted to get to know."

Cormac's smile grew broader. "I like that kid. By the way, I want to get him tickets to our next game." He hesitated, then blurted, "I have a request."

"Shoot."

"I want you to come to the game, too. As my CATS."

"What?"

"We call them CATS—comrades, allies, teammates, spouses. We wanted to differ from other sports that have WAGs, wives and girlfriends. So you'd be my comrade and ally, which leaves teammate and spouse as possible additions." He winked.

"How...very forward thinking of you."

"The name's fun, different, like everything about being in Houston. I like the differences, though. They make us a better team, a more cohesive unit." He peered down at me. "So…will you sit in the CATS section and cheer for me?"

"Are you sure? We've been on one date."

"Two."

I frowned.

"Tonight's our second date. I hope you'll let me make you dinner."

"Make me…" My world kept teetering on its axis, re-righting itself, only to almost spin off again.

"You need to eat, right?"

"Eventually."

"Will you do it with me?" He leaned in closer, running his nose down my cheek, his lips grazing my jaw.

"I'd like that." My voice turned breathy, and my tummy wobbled with pleasure.

"Good. And we'll do another date soon."

"You're sure you want me…" I licked my lips. "You want to be exclusive with me?"

The soft brush of his lips came back up toward mine. Without conscious thought, I turned my head, seeking his mouth.

CHAPTER 12
Cormac

Our lips touched, and electricity blazed between us. My hands dropped to her hips, and my fingers flexed. She was taut but soft, and I gathered her closer, needing more of her taste.

Keelie was special. Whatever happened between us, I was delighted to get to know her, to learn her secrets—that started with her taste. I parted my lips so I could drag my tongue across her lower lip. She opened for me, making a soft, desperate sound even as she pressed closer, crushing her breasts to my chest.

I tipped my head and deepened the kiss, enjoying her flavor as it exploded on my tongue, a headiness curling through my senses. Kissing Keelie jumped to the top of my favorite pastimes.

She wound her arms around my neck, so I lowered one of my arms to under her butt and lifted her. Her legs clasped around my middle, her softness framing my growing hardness, and all the while, our lips and tongues met, tasted, and danced.

Much as I wanted to notch myself into the warm V created by her trim thighs, she mattered too much for me to take this quickly. I didn't want to regret a moment with her. With difficulty, I pulled back, smiling as she sought my lips again.

We finally broke apart, breathing hard. She pressed her fingertips to her lips, her other hand playing with the hair at my nape. I lowered my forehead to touch hers. "To answer your question,

I'm sure I want to be exclusive. After a kiss like that…" I dragged my tongue over my lips, enjoying the hints of Keelie on my tongue. "I'm going to need to kiss you again. And again."

She unhooked her heels from my back and slithered down my body. "I can agree with that."

"Good." I gave her hips a squeeze. "Now, let's commence with this date. What do you want to eat?"

Keelie shrugged. "I'm fairly adventurous. Do you have a diet you need to maintain?"

As I went over my trainer's food suggestions, I preheated the oven and pulled open the freezer.

"These are the pre-made meals my trainer prefers me to eat," I said, waving my hand to showcase the foil-wrapped packages. "But if none of that looks good, we can always cook up some whole-wheat pasta with shrimp."

Her expression lit up at the prospect, but then she pulled out a flaky whitefish meal with herbed sweet potatoes and green beans. That one wasn't my favorite, but it was flavorful, and Keelie seemed intrigued. My chef's helpings were always generous, typically enough for two people—in case I had company. I added it to the oven and set the timer for forty minutes. Then I grabbed her hand.

"Let me show you around." I took her around downstairs, including my home gym that led out onto the pool deck. Many Houston properties had pools, but mine was for laps, so it was a full twenty-five meters long. The stamped concrete surround included an attached hot tub large enough for eight. "I like to sit in there after my cool down. Keeps my muscles loose."

She nodded, dazed. Keelie had said little about her upbringing, but I got the sense her family never had much extra. From her point of view, my lifestyle must be ostentatious, maybe even ridiculous. I glanced over toward the house next door where our goalie, Adam Kramer, lived. Everything about his place was bigger and flashier. I'd become so used to Adam flaunting his wealth, I didn't really see my own.

"Mind if I dip my toes in?" Keelie asked.

"Not at all." I scooted a lounger closer to the edge, and she sat on the side, tugging off her cute cross trainers and ankle socks. Her toenails were bright purple with sparkles. I smiled at the cheerful color.

She rolled up the legs of her jeans and settled on the pool's edge, kicking her feet back and forth.

"This is nice. I don't know that I'd ever leave the deck."

I divested my feet of my socks and shoes and settled next to her. "It's one of the best parts of living here, in such a warm climate. I'm from Toronto and individual pools aren't the norm there. Nor are hot, humid summers."

She nudged my shoulder. "Probably why you're so good at hockey."

I stared out across the water, enjoying the faint hum of cicadas.

"My father put me on skates right after I learned to walk. I wasn't sure I wanted to play hockey—that was his dream—until I won the under-eleven championship. I'm competitive."

She'd turned her face upward and studied me while I spoke. I liked her perusal and how she showed an interest in my past and what I had to say.

"So, you found a passion within your father's dream? Made it your own?"

I shrugged. "Eventually. But the pressure to perform was intense. I moved out at fifteen to billet with another family. That was good, actually, because my father couldn't criticize all my mistakes. It's not that he didn't love me," I rushed to add. "It was just that he expected excellence."

"From a child." She frowned. "I see that often with the parents of my students. It's like people forget the kids are separate people who will have to live their own lives."

We both turned to watch a dragonfly skate over the water's surface. I wondered if Keelie was on to something there. My father had programmed my internal drive for success—I'd never found my passion…or learned how to fail and try something new.

My mother was the same way. She remained hurt by my divorce from Shannon—as if *her* marriage had failed. Only with time and space had I realized how much my parents' expectations smothered me—and that's why I refused to go back to Toronto.

The oven timer chimed via my phone. I stood, letting the water sluice off my calves and feet. "Dinner's ready."

Keelie rose easily and grabbed her shoes and socks in one hand. "Show me where your plates and silverware are, and I'll set the table after I wash my hands."

And just like that, she dropped the tense subject, letting me come back to it in my own way, in my own time. Keelie was so different from anyone else in my life. Possibly because of her profession, but I believed it was *her*—she'd chosen her work based on what suited her best. And she was empathetic but not pushy.

I appreciated that more than she could know, but that didn't mean I wouldn't tell her.

CHAPTER 13
Keelie

I dried my feet with the towel Cormac provided before I padded across the space to where I'd set my phone. Marian had sent me a few texts, as had some of my work colleagues.

This seemed to be part of the cost of dating a professional athlete: other people wanted to get to him through me. I sighed, wondering how I'd know who my genuine, interested-in-me friends were now.

"Everything okay?" Cormac asked. He stood in the kitchen, towel in hand, tall and broad, with sturdy thighs at least twice the size of mine. He turned as he bent to wipe the last of the water from his toes and the floor. His butt was delicious—taut and thick, pure muscle.

I swallowed as need pooled in my abdomen. "How do you handle relationships?" I asked. "I mean, already people are messaging me because they want to meet you."

Cormac put out his hand for my towel, which I gave him. He gripped both his towel and mine in one hand as he eased in close enough to touch my cheek. "The part of fame I dislike most is the loss of anonymity. People talk, and they're not all nice. Some people will try to use you, and that hurts. But I promise you this, Keelie: I'll do everything I can to protect you, to let you know how much I respect and cherish you."

I raised my eyebrows. "Cherish? I must be a fine communicator if we're there already." My belly buzzed with nerves as I tried to keep it light. I squashed the yearning down.

He tapped the tip of my nose with his finger. "It's the sass. I can't get enough of it."

The timer chimed again, so he turned away to get the food from the oven. "Dishes are there, glasses there, and silverware there." He pointed with his free hand. "I'm going to throw these in the laundry room."

"Sounds good." After washing my hands, I refilled our glasses and grabbed silverware, then set everything on the table. It was some hardwood I wasn't familiar with—seemed solid, not a veneer like mine.

"How hungry are you?" he asked as he pulled out a serving spoon.

"Hungry. I run after kids all day."

Cormac dished up some of the flaky fish and settled it next to the vegetables he'd already put on my plate. "Definitely burning some calories."

"Not as many as you."

"Few people in the world push themselves physically like I do," he said. "I like to work out—keeps me from being antsy."

He piled his own plate high.

"Are you typically antsy?"

"I have a hard time settling my mind. Movement helps me focus both my body and my thoughts."

"That doesn't mean you're antsy, just that you use your body to feel your thoughts and emotions."

He nodded thoughtfully as he carried the plates to the table and pulled out a chair, gesturing for me to sit.

"Thanks." I settled into the seat.

"That's an interesting concept," Cormac said, pulling the paper napkin dispenser closer and offering me one before taking another for himself.

I met his gaze. The brown in his eyes was luscious, like hot cocoa. I adored cocoa—chocolate in all its forms. "Because it's not the typical statement about ADHD?"

"Yeah."

He picked up his utensils and cut into his fish, so I did the same. "Mmm... This is so good," I exclaimed, placing my hand in front of my mouth. I blushed, embarrassed at my poor manners, but *damn*. I hadn't known boring old whitefish could be so tasty.

"I have a talented chef."

I shook my head. Once I'd swallowed, I said, "Tell me about this chef."

"She comes in twice a week and makes meals based on what the team nutritionist recommends."

I set my utensils down and cupped my chin in my palm. "And that's your normal?"

"It is." He took another bite.

I liked his economical, precise movements. "I cook my boring recipes like meatloaf, hoping I can stretch it another day so I can add another fifty bucks to my student loans—that's normal."

"For you."

"For most of the world."

"I'm not most people," he said.

"Noted."

He pointed his knife at me. "You going to let it get cold?"

"No."

We ate, moving from one topic to another.

"Who doesn't like NWA or Nirvana?" Cormac asked a little way into our music discussion, clearly affronted.

"This girl," I said, laughing. "I grew up on the classics: Tammy Wynette, Merle Haggard. I like good ol' country."

Cormac shook his head, grumbling. He finished his meal and leaned back in his chair, hands over his flat tummy. "That may be a deal breaker."

I aligned the silverware on my plate. "That's the end? Me liking country music?"

"Maybe."

"Have you ever listened to it?"

"No."

"Then how can you know you don't like it?"

He opened his mouth, closed it, then shrugged. "Because it's twangy?"

I chortled. "I'll turn you yet. You wait."

Cormac leaned forward, expression serious. "I don't doubt that for a minute. Not with what I'm feeling."

And then he kissed me. This moment proved different from the make-out session earlier and from our first featherlight perfection.

This kiss said, *I know what you like.* I know to nibble here and lick there. I know you, and I enjoy making you hot and bothered… And I want to do more of that.

I melted against him, my fingers gripping his biceps and soft moans issuing from my throat. Sure, Cormac lived in a fancy house and ate fancy food prepared by a fancy chef, but it was *his* touch—his kisses, specifically—that caused me to lose my mind and want to give him everything I had.

Something told me that the more time I spent with this man, the more willing I'd be to slide into his foreign world.

CHAPTER 14

Cormac

I slapped my alarm, growling at its beeping. I finally raised my head and opened my eyes enough to turn it off before I flopped back against my pillow, wanting to return to sleep…until I remembered my night with Keelie.

I smiled as warm fuzzies blossomed in my chest. She was so cute. Funny, but with wit—not coarse humor like Cruz. I craved more of that, along with her empathy.

When she'd insisted she head home last night, I'd been disappointed. Sure, I knew she had work to do in the kids' files, which she'd told me, but I still hadn't wanted her to leave. For the first time in ages, I'd felt as if my house was a home. I'd missed that feeling of belonging. I grabbed my phone and sent Keelie a text.

Morning, beautiful. I hope you have a great day making kids' lives better. I'm going to practice. See you at five at your place.

I'd asked her if I could come over today to see her DIYed ceiling, and she'd agreed. Three dots appeared and a moment later, she replied: *Morning! I'm on my second cup of coffee and about to head into the classroom.*

Don't let those rugrats push you around.

I smiled throughout practice, and not even Cruz's surliness dampened my mood. But the message from my mother that I received after practice did.

"Cormac, what is this I hear about you seeing a woman?" her voicemail began.

She spoke in French, her preferred language. Because of her frustration and disdain, she sounded much more nasally than usual.

"You are bound still to Shannon. You took vows in the church. How can you turn your back on your wife like so?"

She continued her tirade, but I'd heard it all before. Still, my mother's words left me unsettled, annoyed. Much as I wanted to call her back and respond with my anger, that would solve nothing. My parents were good people—honest, hardworking... naïve.

I wouldn't change them, not now, so the best I could do was learn to accept them as they were. Not a simple task, and another reason I didn't visit often.

Late that afternoon, I left the rink and stopped at the store to buy Keelie flowers—big, bold sunflowers because they reminded me of her smile. Then I drove on to the address she'd given me.

I pulled into her narrow driveway in a residential area about ten miles from the Medical Center and the Galleria. Built in the early fifties, each of the neighborhood's ranch-style houses had a brick façade and a jewel-green grassy yard with a few trees. The garages were behind the homes, detached and less convenient for bringing in cold items during the months-long summer.

I headed up the front path, noting the cracked concrete where a tree's root must have risen too close to the surface—not an uncommon issue in the city. The flowerbed surrounding her large oak bloomed with a variety of flowers, mostly pinks, lavenders, and light blues. I wasn't knowledgeable about the blooms, but they were pretty. Keelie took pride in her home and her space. I reached the front and knocked on the glass storm door. Keelie and a cat greeted me—Keelie with a kiss, the cat with a meow. I loved the kiss.

"Mmm... I like that greeting," I murmured against her lips.

She smiled even as she kissed me again. Being with Keelie was so natural, so *right*. I didn't know how else to explain it.

"Who's this?" I asked, charmed by the pretty gray-and-white cat. Big green eyes stared at me, unblinking. "These are for you," I added, holding out the bouquet.

"Oooh, thanks. I've never received flowers before," Keelie said. "That's Slippers."

I noted both her comment about flowers—I planned to correct that often—and the cat's white paws.

"She showed up one day after a thunderstorm."

I lowered to one knee. Slippers surprised me by sniffing my fingers and then shoving her head under them.

"She's affectionate," Keelie said.

"I noticed." I petted her head, pleased by her purr. "The ceiling looks good."

Keelie chuckled. "A little sweat equity goes a long way. Well, that, too many hours of home-improvement videos, and friend-shaming."

"Friend-shaming?" I asked with a frown. I made to rise, but Slippers scooted forward and placed a dainty paw on my thigh.

"Marian. My friend. She hated my popcorn ceiling even more than I did."

I narrowed my eyes. "So she helped you?"

"Nope. Marian doesn't do chores." Keelie moved toward the kitchen where she found a vase and arranged her flowers. That done, she opened her fridge, biting her lip.

"She didn't help you?" I pressed.

"Nope. Well, she brought supplies, then baited me into getting started."

Didn't sound like much of a friend to me.

"Are you hungry? How about a big green salad with chicken?"

"Sounds good. Can I help?"

She shook her head. "I don't like to share my kitchen."

My eyebrows rose. Keelie seemed so laid back, thoughtful, so for her to be territorial... "How long have you been cooking?"

She shrugged. "Since before I can remember. My mother's not much of a cook, and I enjoyed eating, so..."

Another piece of her personality, her history. I might not get along with my parents, but we'd lived a well-to-do lifestyle because of my father's executive-level position at a major aviation firm. My mother had stayed at home to provide the best opportunities for me when I was young, and when I was a little older, to drive me to all my hockey practices and games. My father loved watching me play, so he'd come to nearly every event, even after I moved out at fifteen.

"What kept you in Houston?" I asked. I finally rose as Slippers slunk away. She jumped lightly onto a windowsill and laid down, her bushy, white-tipped tail swaying back and forth in a lazy pendulum. I crossed the space and washed my hands.

Keelie glanced up at me from where she was slicing a pear.

She'd set a hunk of bleu cheese on her counter, next to tart cherries, walnuts, and a bag of baby greens. She heated a pan, then surprised me by tossing in a couple handfuls of nuts. "Why would I go somewhere else?" she asked. "Houston is one of the largest cities in the country with tons of culture, art, you name it."

"You like art?"

"Museums are fabulous. So is the ballet."

I smiled. "You like ballet?"

She removed the toasted nuts and laid two chicken breasts in the pan. "I wanted to be a ballerina. But then, so do most little girls. They also want a pony."

"I like being here too, and I was glad for the opportunity to move away from my parents. They're stifling."

"How so?"

I considered her as I leaned against the counter's edge. "I guess…their expectations, which I mentioned before. They put all the time and effort into my hockey, so I needed to get drafted, and then I needed to be the best at my position. When I married Shannon, my mother expected grandbabies…" I shook my head. "She's still upset that Shannon and I divorced. She's a devout Catholic."

A funny expression crossed Keelie's face. "That might explain it," she murmured.

"Explain what?"

She shook her head. "It's not important. Tell me more about your family."

I didn't like her changing the subject, but I let it go. I snagged a bite of pear as I considered what to tell her.

"My mom miscarried when I was four. I don't remember that part, but I remember the aftermath—how she was so sad and needed to stay in bed. She couldn't have more kids after that."

"Did she want more?"

"Yeah, she and my dad had wanted a large family. They got me." I shrugged like it didn't matter, but it did—the weight of all their hopes and dreams rested on my shoulders, and I'd never quite been able to live up to them. "So my mom's been desperate for grandkids. As soon as they realized my career in the NHL was going to last—as long as I don't get injured—my mother started asking."

Keelie nodded. "And you said that wasn't something Shannon was interested in. Starting a family." She slid the cooked chicken onto a cutting board before moving back to put the salad together in a large bowl.

"Nope. Shan never wanted kids, but she didn't tell me that until we'd already gotten married. For a while, I was in denial, but once I saw how much the idea worried her, I said it didn't matter; we just wouldn't have kids."

Her expression softened. "Because you loved her."

Nodding, I said, "I did, and for a while I thought she might come around. I also wanted to be true to my vows. When she asked for a divorce, I was angry—no, furious. I'd been willing to sacrifice my dreams of a family for her, but she wouldn't do the same for me. She said she was 'setting me free' but she's never entirely left my life. After a while, we became friends again. Lately I've noticed that she checks up on me, makes sure I'm not dating anyone."

"Could be her, then," she muttered.

"What's that?"

Keelie met my gaze and chewed her lip. Finally, she slid her phone out of her pocket. After pressing some buttons, she turned the phone to face me. "Listen to that message."

I didn't know the number, but I did as she said. My eyebrows rose. "That's…wow. And you thought that could be *Shannon?*" She was still gnawing on her lip. I tugged it free.

"Or your mom," she said.

"I'm glad you told me. Can I take a screenshot of this?"

"Sure. Do you know who it is?"

"Yeah." I blew out a breath. "It's my mother."

We were silent for a moment. Then Keelie cleared her throat. "Dinner's ready. That is…if you still want to eat with me."

I frowned. "Why wouldn't I?"

She placed her hands flat on the counter next to my hip. "There are some strong headwinds fighting against us."

I wrapped my arms around her waist and tugged her close. "There's something you need to know about me: when I see something I want, I go after it."

She smiled. "You're so intense. But I don't understand why me."

She'd asked me before, but this time I had an answer. I skimmed my fingertips down her cheek before settling my thumb against her lower lip. "Your smile. The way your eyes light up. The way you make me feel." I relished the heat of her body. "I don't know what it is exactly, but I feel alive when I'm with you. And I like the feeling. Actually, I'm addicted to it. There's something about you I can't seem to live without."

CHAPTER 15
Keelie

I continued to hold Cormac's gaze, trying to read him. "That's… something."

"Dating me will be hard sometimes, and I don't want fake tabloid stories, my mother, or my ex-wife to get between us. I want to be happy, and I'll be happiest with you."

I swallowed but pressed a kiss to his thumb. "I still don't get why you like me, but I'm glad you do."

"For now, can that be enough?" Cormac asked, his expression yearning, willing me to accept.

"Yes."

"Great," he said with a sigh. "Now can we eat? I'm starving."

I laughed as I stepped away. "Sure can. Let me get some plates."

We ate, enjoying the meal and each other's company. After dinner, he insisted on cleaning up, and I wouldn't argue. Sure, I liked to load my dishwasher a certain way, but I liked not having to do all the dishes even more. I wiped the counters and table while he washed the skillet.

"All done," he said, setting it in the drain tray. He turned around, catching me admiring his butt. He grinned.

"What can I say?" I fluttered my lashes at him. "All that skating clearly pays off."

He sauntered toward me. "I have great stamina."

Desire smoldered in my belly. "I bet you do."

He placed one hand on the right side of my body and the other on the left, caging me between his thick forearms and chest, the counter at my back. I wiggled forward so I was plastered against him, one of his heavy thighs between mine. My chest fizzed with anticipation as I tipped my face up. He caught the back of my head with his hand, cupping my skull.

He was so big, so capable. So warm and safe. I never felt truly safe—not ever. I tried not to dwell on how much my dad's rejection had messed me up, so when tears formed, I blinked them back. "Cormac?"

"Yes?"

"Will you…" I dragged my tongue along my lower lip. His gaze followed the action, and his eyes flared with heat. He pressed his thigh upward a little, lifting me to my tiptoes. More heat somersaulted through my core. "Kiss me?" I breathed.

His lips brushed over mine. He liked to tease, damn him. I caught his cheeks between my palms and turned my head, lips devouring his. He grunted, his fingers tightening against my skull I met his second thrust by wrapping my tongue around his and sucking hard. He growled. I pressed my chest tighter against him. He nipped my lips, and I rubbed my breasts across the thick slab of muscle that was his chest.

Each move and countermove inflamed me more. I whimpered into his mouth. Cormac deepened the kiss further. My panties grew damp as my need skyrocketed and my nerve endings sparked, sensitized to his touch. I tore my mouth from his, chest heaving. "I…"

He gathered me closer, shifting my body to press me against the bulge between his legs. He widened his stance and used his hips to grind us together. I gasped at the friction, fingers scrambling for purchase as my head fell back, my mind blanking of anything but how good he felt rubbing against me.

He set me down as he shook his head. "Too fast... I can't think. I need...*fuck*."

He stumbled back, somehow being careful with me. He rested his hands on his thighs and heaved a breath—like I'd seen sprinters do after an arduous run.

I wanted—needed—to know so much more about him, but I wanted to throw myself into his arms and beg him to make me his. The conflicting emotions swirled through me, causing my head to ache nearly as much as the tender place between my thighs. "I'm sorry."

He lifted his head, eyes wild but mouth set. "Don't apologize. If you need more time, you have it."

Playing with a thick chunk of my hair, I didn't look up. "It's not so much about need as it is concern. I'm on the pill, but... but...what if... What if I got pregnant?" The words rushed past my lips.

Cormac rose to his full height and stared down at me. "If you were pregnant, I'd be happy. No, *thrilled*." Sincerity radiated from him.

I laid my hand on his chest. "You don't get it," I whispered. For a long moment, I hesitated. "I grew up in a broken home. I don't want to do that to my baby." That's as close as I could get right now to telling him about my father's betrayal.

His hand clasped mine. "It's a hypothetical right now. To be fair, I worried over this last weekend, but seeing you again has solidified something for me. I want you in my life, Keelie." He smiled. "So I stand by my statement. I'd be thrilled to take care of our baby and you, sweet girl." He pressed a kiss to my temple. Then he stepped back. "I'm going to go."

I nodded, sadness coloring the edges of my consciousness because I wanted him to stay and cuddle with me on the couch. I wanted him to spend the night...and I didn't. So fast. This was all happening so quickly. I couldn't get my bearings, catch my breath. I tugged harder at the ends of my hair. "You're sure you can't stay? For a little while?"

He brushed my hair back from my forehead and kissed my hairline. "If I stay, I'm going to want to be inside you."

I shivered, shocked by how pleased his words made me. He was gentle with me but also bold to the point of domineering. He didn't cross the line, just toed up to it, and that side of him fascinated me. Cormac...was the alpha of the pack. As captain of a professional hockey team, I guess I should have realized he'd dominate most people in a room—heck, the *world*. But he never pushed me, not even now, when I knew he wanted more.

He tipped my chin up. "You'll come to my game tomorrow?"

"Oh. Oh...yes, that...*wow*." I grinned. "That would be amazing. I've never been to a hockey game."

"Do you have a friend you can bring? I don't want you to be lonely."

"Are you sure? I don't want to cause any problems."

"I have an allotted number of tickets per game. Consider

them yours indefinitely."

I rose on my tiptoes and brushed my lips over his. "Thank you."

He gripped my hips for a moment before he sighed. "Goodnight, Keelie. Sleep sweet."

I hated that he walked away, though it was for the best. Once my door was closed and locked, I leaned against it. Groaning, I tugged my phone from my pocket. I dialed Marian, though part of me didn't want to share this with her. *Maybe I should call Lisa instead.*

"Hello?"

Too late to second-guess my choice.

"Want to join me for the Wildcatters game tomorrow?" I asked instead of a greeting.

"Hell yeah, I do! Are we going to be sitting in a certain someone's section?"

"Cormac offered me his tickets, yes."

"Bring a change of clothes," Marian said. "Cute ones. You're not going to the game in your teacher garb."

"What's wrong with my clothes?" I demanded.

"Everything. They're baggy—"

"Comfortable."

"Old, even threadbare—"

"So I don't have to worry about paints or other things the kids spill on them."

"Yeah, exactly. You need to wear something cute, not covered in glue and snot."

I sighed, and we chatted for a few minutes, but I hung up,

frowning. Even for Marian, that comment went too far. I sighed, shaking my head. Much as I didn't want to admit it, she and I were growing apart. And I *definitely* should have called Lisa to be my plus-one.

CHAPTER 16
Cormac

Nerves fluttered in my belly, but I tamped them down and lifted my chest, then my chin. As captain of the team, the guys needed me to be a solid presence. Still, my guts shifted and rolled.

"What's with you?" Cruz, the hulking defenseman, asked.

"I don't know." *Fuck*. This was weird. I didn't understand what was going on inside me.

He grabbed my chin, his rough, callused fingers scraping against the bristles I hadn't bothered to shave off.

"You're *nervous*," he said. His eyes widened. "Is someone hurt? What don't we know?"

Other guys stopped what they were doing, the talking died down, and everyone turned to face me. I gritted my teeth.

"Nothing's new with New York. We play the game the way Coach laid it out for us."

"He *does* look nervous," Nik said. He peered at me. "Green around the edges. Are you going to puke?"

I rose unsteadily. "Enough! I'm fine—"

"Just freaking out that the girl he likes finally agreed to come to the game." Maxim offered a smirk as he adjusted his sweater.

"After one date she's *your girl*?" Nik asked.

"Three dates." I pressed my hand to my stomach. "I don't want to embarrass myself."

Nik, Stol, Cruz, and Maxim gaped at me. "Embarrass..." Cruz mouthed.

"He *really* likes her," Maxim added. "And it's screwing with his head." He gestured toward me. "Obviously."

"You're a sadistic bastard," I said. "You liked that she scolded you."

"That was *hot*..." Maxim rubbed his hand across his scruffy cheek.

"You took Maxim to meet her?" Nik pulled back, shock and hurt on his face.

I shrugged. "He's the guy who dropped my phone in Cruz's ice bath, so I couldn't call her."

Nik's fists clenched. "I would have vouched for you." His accent thickened.

"I was going to ask if you wanted to meet her after the game," I said to fill the heavy silence.

"You could have told your closest friends," Cruz sniffed. He turned back to his locker, hurt radiating from him. Nik followed suit.

My stomach rolled again. Arguing with the guys about my romantic life was...*weird*. Their investment freaked me out.

I turned and puked in the helmet in front of the locker next to mine.

"Gross." Maxim scrambled back.

I wiped my mouth with the back of my hand. "That's what you get for tattling and getting me in trouble."

The rest of the guys went back to their pregame routines, but Cruz shot me a small smile and Nik a wink. My stomach calmed, and I rose, heading to the bathroom to wash out my mouth.

We skated out through the smokescreen and onto our side of the ice, the speakers blaring our names and the crowd roaring for their favorites. I skated forward, arms lifted, as the announcer called my name. I zeroed in on my seats. Keelie was clapping, her mouth open in a yell. My stomach settled, and the tension ebbed from my neck.

I shot her a wink and a smile. Then I shook out my arms and turned my focus to the game.

"You good?" Maxim asked as we stood in line for the national anthem. He'd gotten a different helmet from our equipment manager.

"I'm good."

"Your girl should wear your number."

I glanced at Keelie. *Hell, yeah, she should.* "I'll take care of it."

"And her. Take care of her." Maxim lifted his face to the flag, effectively ending our conversation.

We skated to our bench, and Coach Whittaker frowned at me. "Heard you were sick. Do I need to pull you?"

I shook my head. "All's good now."

He raised an eyebrow but let it go, calling in the rest of the first line and going over his initial plan of attack.

The line hit the ice, taking their positions. Nik slammed his stick down at center ice, his face fierce with concentration. The puck dropped. I skated forward, using every bit of muscle in my legs to propel me ahead of my opponent. The puck sailed across the ice to the other side of the rink, skimming against the boards before Maxim isolated it and shot it across the ice. He took a hard hit. Setting my jaw, I planned to get even with New York's defenseman, but first I needed to accept the puck. Some quick legwork and chopping motions with my stick kept my D-man off the puck until I caught sight of Nik open. I passed the puck to him, and he maneuvered the rest of the way up the ice, passing it off to Cruz, who lobbed it back. Nik popped the shot around the edge of the net, just squeaking it past their goalie's glove.

Blue light bloomed, and the horn sounded. Less than five minutes into the first period, and we had ourselves a goal.

I glanced over at Keelie, who stood and cheered.

I'd forgotten how good it felt to have someone in the stands.

CHAPTER 17
Keelie

I settled back in my seat, flushed with excitement, chest heaving from yelling. I took a long gulp of the beer Marian had brought back, wincing at its yeastiness but thankful for the cooling sensation as it slid down my burning throat. I hadn't yelled this much in ages—maybe ever.

"Hockey's exciting," I said.

Marian shot me a rueful look. "More so when you're emotionally invested in one player."

"I'm not sure where this is going." I knew where I wanted my relationship with Cormac to go—if I could learn to trust him.

She shrugged. "You don't have to be sure. You just have to enjoy."

Tonight, she'd smiled when she arrived and seemed happy to see me. Maybe she was just having a rough time lately. I understood people taking out their negativity on others; my mother did that, often, and I refused to talk to her when she treated me like her punching bag.

I mulled over Marian's words as I watched the opposing team make a run toward the Wildcatters' goalie. I gasped as the player hauled back and slapped a shot. Adam sprawled out in the split, the puck slamming into his padded thigh before he grabbed it in his mitted hands. I pressed my palm to my racing heart. This game might be *too* exciting.

The period ended with the Wildcatters up one-nil, and the crowd heaved as one to stand and march back up the aisles to the restrooms or to purchase more concessions from the wide array of overpriced options. The Zamboni slid out of its gate and began a leisurely re-glazing of the ice.

I tugged my cardigan tighter around my torso as I leaned forward and touched Andy's shoulder. "Having fun?"

He nodded as he beamed, his gap-toothed smile wider than I'd ever seen it.

"Ms. Hayes?" I turned, surprised to find a young woman in khakis and a Wildcatter polo standing nearby. "Cormac wanted to make sure you brought Andy back to the locker room after the game." She glanced at Andy's father. "As long as you're okay with that, sir."

I waited for Andy's father to communicate with his son. He gave me a nod, his smile matching Andy's, before I agreed.

"Great! I'll come back to collect you all afterward," the woman said. "Enjoy the rest of the game."

Marian smiled, seeming gleeful at the prospect. People around us pulled out their phones, snapping pictures…of *me*. One older gentleman sitting a row behind and to the left reached forward and tapped my shoulder.

I glanced back, unsure about the sudden attention and whispering. "Yes?"

"You know Cormac Bouchard?"

I cleared my dry throat. "I do." My palms sweat. What if this guy asked about my relationship with him? What if he… I frowned. Why was I worried about what others thought of me? Didn't I teach my kids to be strong and confident in their choices?

"Tell him he's a second too slow. We won't get to the championships if he doesn't pick up his game."

"I'll tell him," I said, my tone as dry as my mouth.

CHAPTER 18
Cormac

"Great game," I said, clapping Nik, then Cruz on the shoulder. Maxim was too far ahead to congratulate. "I invited Keelie down here. I'm not sure if she can come to the restaurant. She has to teach school tomorrow."

"You're dating a teacher?" Adam cracked up and slid off the bench.

I scowled, but before I could say anything, Maxim nudged Adam with the edge of his skate. "She's awesome, dude. Now shut up and sign this sweater. We're giving it to one of her students. Kid's cute but has some kind of motor issue, and I think he's bullied."

That shut Adam up—his younger sister had been bullied in school to the point she'd hurt herself. He grabbed the marker and signed. "What else are we doing for this kid?" he asked, all business.

"Keelie looks out for him, and we invited him here. The sweater's another level of security—"

"I'll visit him at lunch," Adam said. "Sit with him. Make sure the other students know he's my bud."

Maxim scratched his beard. "That's a good idea. Why didn't I think of that?"

"Because you don't think," Nik said. He whipped off his

sweater and unlaced his skates. He lifted his head and glared at me. "You introduce me to your girl."

I smiled. "Will do."

"Well, if I think she's cool, I expect you to lock her down."

I rolled my eyes. We didn't always agree on how to talk about—or to—women, but the guys had good hearts.

"What happens if I don't get your seal of approval?" I peeled off my sweater, pads, and undershirt, throwing them all in the bin that would go to the center's laundry facility.

"Lucky for you, you have mine," Maxim called over his shoulder. "That's the only one that matters."

"I'll let you know my thoughts," Cruz rumbled from his bench.

I shook my head as I finished stripping. The shower area had filled with steam by the time I entered. I went to my usual spot and turned the handle, groaning as the hot water speared into my battered muscles. Now that I was in my thirties, nothing healed as quickly as it had when I was an eighteen-year-old rookie. That's why I had to play smarter than the new kids. I typically did.

I winced, cupping a deep bruise on my right ribs. The hit by the opposing D-man late in the third period smarted—in part because it had allowed New York to score a goal, but also because he'd hammered me with his shoulder, and then his stick. The ref hadn't seen that, just as he'd intended.

I washed my hair and body, then toweled off, not wanting to keep Keelie or Andy waiting. Once I stepped into my street clothes—nice slacks, argyle socks (because everyone needed some style), dress shoes, and a button-down shirt—I ran a comb through my damp hair and grabbed my bag, phone, wallet, and keys from their spots in my locker.

Cruz was already gone, and so was Maxim. I picked up the pace, wincing as my bruised ribs protested. I burst through the doors into the concrete hallway to find six of the guys lining up to take a photo with Andy.

"Cormac! Yay! Now we can take it." Andy beamed at me.

I hustled over, planning to give him a high-five, but he rammed into my legs, wrapping his arms as far around my thighs as he could. I stroked his back as Keelie stepped up next to me.

"Want me to hold your bag?" she asked.

I handed her the bag and used that arm to clasp the back of her neck under the heavy weight of her hair. I pulled her closer and kissed her temple, inhaling her sweet fragrance. The woman Keelie had been sitting with glared at me, then at Keelie. Naked jealousy blared from her expression.

I refocused on Keelie. She wore Wildcatters red and silver, a pretty red shirt with a little frill at the collar and a silver cardigan to keep her warm. That was Keelie—sensible but soft. I admired her trim legs in her jeans and enjoyed the moment, soaking in her warmth, even as I rubbed Andy's back. He talked a mile a minute, clearly keyed up to meet the team.

"You look good like that, Mac," Maxim said. "You ought to get yourself a family."

I pulled back enough to look into Keelie's wide blue eyes. Her pink cheeks were as adorable as her shocked expression. She was gorgeous. I already had a ridiculous obsession with the faint freckles that sprinkled her forehead—right where I liked to kiss her. Her lips beckoned me—slick and pink with just the right plumpness to press into…or bite.

I smiled at her before I bent down and collected Andy. I walked to the center of the group of guys and smiled for the picture as my mind stuck on how much I'd love to be holding my kid right now—mine and Keelie's.

CHAPTER 19
Keelie

Cormac slid his hand against mine, fingers squeezing gently as he walked me down the now-quiet hallway toward his exit. Nik, the defenseman we'd been talking to, hurried on ahead.

"Did you drive?" Cormac asked.

I shook my head. "Marian drove. My car's at my house."

"Good. That means I get to give you a ride." He lifted our joined hands and kissed my knuckle.

Last I'd seen her, Marian was talking to Cormac's friend Maxim, but they'd since disappeared. I would have sent Marian a text, but she didn't like me to "hover." In fact, as soon as we'd come down here, she'd gone back to making biting comments toward and about me.

Unsure what to do about her behavior, I'd chosen not to press the issue. But that had butterflies tumbling through my mid-section. I hated confrontation. *Hated*. It.

Still, I couldn't let Marian walk all over my feelings. Something would have to change.

"Do you know what happened to Marian?" I asked.

Cormac pursed his lips. "Yeah."

I raised my eyebrows in question. He sighed. "She propositioned Max. He declined. She…didn't take that well."

My brows pinched. "Oh, no."

"Are you two close?" Cormac asked.

Another wave of discontent rolled through me. "We met in college. She never had many friends. I know she can be sharp…" I turned to face him. "I'm sorry she embarrassed Maxim."

"Your friend stomped off, but she didn't seem overly upset. I planned to tell you."

"Okay. Thanks. What about Maxim?"

"Max doesn't get embarrassed. At least I've never seen it. And don't worry. We've all had practice turning down women." He glanced at me from the corner of his eye. "Some of us way more than others."

"Hmmm…"

"For the record, you're the only woman I want to spend time with." He raised our clasped hands and kissed mine again.

Desire ignited there and spread outward. "Okay."

We walked along in silence. My concern weighing on the moment. "You sure you don't want to go to the bar with your teammates?" I asked.

"I'm sure. I'm right where I want to be."

This man charmed me so effortlessly.

"Thank you for coming tonight," he said. "Having you in the stands, cheering for me…that meant a lot."

I practically bounced along next to him as I relived the goal he'd scored, my excitement shoving aside my concerns about Marian. "Are you kidding? That was so exciting! Man, the adrenaline rush."

He smiled, his face partially in shadows. "Did you play sports as a kid?"

My good mood fizzled a bit. "I mean, the ones at school. I

was very good at dodgeball."

"You seem like you have a favorite sport. Let's hear it."

I released a long breath. "I always wanted to play golf."

"Golf? Huh. I would have pictured you as a runner or a swimmer."

With a shrug, I said, "I tried both—casually in elementary school before you had to pay all the money for select teams. I ran some in college because they gave me a scholarship, but we didn't have enough extra money for swimming fees for me to be on a private team, so it wasn't ever really an option."

"I knew you were a runner."

I frowned. "How?"

"Those sexy legs." He leered at my lower half.

I laughed.

"And I saw your trophies," Cormac said.

That made more sense.

"Isn't golf pricey?" He squeezed my hand gently, as if to soften the blow.

"It is. I've only played a few times, but I love it. I love being outside, the strategy, the different clubs, whacking the ball—all of it."

He smiled. "I bet you're cute in a golf shirt and those weird knicker thingies they wear."

I laughed. "I wouldn't know. I don't have a golf wardrobe."

He spun me around, wrapping his arms around my waist. His nose nuzzled my neck. "Go with me."

"What?"

He walked us backward until my back pressed against the wall of the tunnel, mere feet from the double-door exit.

"Let me take you to play golf. We'll go on your next day off."

"Don't you have games on the weekends?"

"Yes, we're traveling this coming weekend." He grimaced. "And a good chunk of next week. But we're back Thursday. Let me take you to play golf."

Licking my lips as I raised my hands, I settled my palms on his warm, thick biceps. I resisted the urge to squeeze the firm muscle. "I have next Friday off. Teacher in-service."

He trailed his lips up my neck and across my cheek toward my lips. "Perfect. We'll hit the links, and I'll take you to lunch after. Then we can go back to my place for some time in the pool and hot tub. Sound okay?"

It sounded amazing. "Y-yes."

He kissed me. Cormac, I'd found, liked to seduce me with his lips, but also with his large hands and even his thick thighs. He lifted me, and my legs wound around his waist. He pressed me against the concrete wall of the tunnel, his hips settled into the V of my spread thighs. His lips glided over mine as he nibbled, licked, and nuzzled. I slid my fingers into the hair at the back of his neck and held on, tilting my head to give him better access to my mouth. He moaned and pressed himself more firmly against my core.

"Oh, Keelie," he murmured, expression darkening with heat and promise. "What I want to do with you…" He pulled back, letting me ease my legs to the ground. He took my hand once more and kissed the back again. "But I'll start with another date and kicking your ass at golf."

CHAPTER 20
Cormac

I missed Keelie that night after I'd dropped her at home, so I texted her before I fell asleep.

Her response was waiting for me in the morning: *I like holding you, Cormac. But I like kissing you more.*

I grinned as I sauntered into my bathroom to get ready for our morning skate. Then the team would fly out for a four-day road trip.

On the way to the arena, Keelie texted me again. After I parked, I checked my phone. A pleased smile flashed across my face as I saw the photo of her crouched down, her cheek pressed to Andy's as he held up the sweater we'd signed.

Maxim tapped on my window, so I opened the door, snagging my keys and bag. "Looks like we did some good work last night."

"We fucking owned New York—awwwww..." Maxim's face melted into soft goo as he took in the picture.

"That face better be for the cute kid and not my girl."

"She's sexy, but he's awesome."

As I chuckled, I relaxed. I needed to get a grip. Jealousy was a new feeling for me—maybe because I was *the* catch in high school when Shannon and I started dating. I scowled as I fell into step next to Cruz. Shannon had remained faithful until we'd separated, and I believed her when she'd told me she still loved me. Granted, we'd been finalizing our divorce, but she hadn't pushed for any of my money or investments. I'd given her the condo, and she still lived there, but she'd left our marriage with only what she'd brought to it. I respected her for that.

But not for fucking Dukovsky. I'd never forgive her for that. Nor him.

"What's that look for? I thought you were all heart-and-flowers over the teacher," Nik said, bumping my shoulder.

"He is," Maxim said.

I stopped walking, so they both paused, too, expressions full of anticipation. "What if she's like my ex? What if I just can't see it?"

"We like her—right now," Maxim said. "If we got weird vibes, we'd tell you."

"Good." I blew out a breath. "It's been a long time…"

"We know," Nik said. He fake shuddered. "That's a long damn time to go without the goods."

I cracked a smile even as I shook my head. "She's more than sex to me." And that still surprised me somehow. The attraction between us had been strong, instantaneous, but I really enjoyed spending time with her.

"Why?" Nik cried. His expression turned plaintive. "Why can't you just have fun?"

We started walking again as I considered his question. Just before we hit the doors to the locker room, I said, "I like to be connected emotionally to the woman in my bed."

Nik shot me a confused look, making a choked sound, but Maxim nodded before he took off toward his locker.

The moment we landed after our trip, I drove to Keelie's place and enjoyed snuggling with her and Slippers.

"I like this," I said. I pressed a kiss to her temple as I ran a hand down Slippers' sleek side.

"I like this, too," she said, tipping her head back. She licked her lips, and I took her up on the invitation.

When I pulled back, we were both breathless. I touched her plump lower lip. "I should go. We have practice and you have to work."

Sadness rounded her shoulders, but she nodded. "Okay."

"Eventually you're going to stop kicking me out," I joked.

Her eyes widened. "I'm not kicking you out."

"I know."

She lowered her lashes. "I'll tell you why I want to take this slow. Soon."

I pulled her into my arms. I heard the pain lacing her words. "When you're ready." I rested my chin on the crown of her head. For a long moment, I soaked up the joy of holding her. Then, with a sigh, I kissed her cheek and stepped away. "I'll see you soon."

She fisted my shirt. "I'm going to miss you," she whispered. "From the moment you leave."

"I'll miss you, too." Some women hated the professional-athlete schedule and refused to date men who were gone so much of the season. We'd already gone through one trial. We had another on its heels because we had another road series coming up soon. I kissed Keelie again, silently begging her not to push me away.

Our schedules were busy the rest of the week and didn't mesh, so we texted back and forth every day. She sent me pictures of

Slippers and of her new DIY project—a raised garden bed. On the plane for our next away game, I researched the best do-it-yourself projects for us to tackle. Maybe I'd make an outdoor conversation area in my yard, where we could string lights. When I sent Keelie the idea later that night, she called me back. We'd arrived at the hotel, and I had just settled into the room.

As she wound down on her list of ideas, I continued to smile up at the ceiling. "What were you doing?"

"Nothing. Well, moping, I guess. Marian and I watch *The Witcher* together on Tuesdays."

I pressed my lips together, not wanting to disparage Keelie's friend. "And…?"

"She didn't show. So I got a whole pizza—just for me." Her laugh strained at the edges. "I'm going to have to talk to her—I know that. It's just…"

"I'm sorry, sweet girl. You deserve better."

I wanted to call Marian and yell at her for making Keelie sad. More, I wanted to call her and tell her to fuck off and never bother Keelie again. Neither was a viable option, which left me feeling out of sorts.

Keelie sighed. "I wish you were here to give me a hug."

"Me, too."

After a moment, she brightened. "I'm sorry. I didn't say great game tonight! That goal was amazing!" she gushed.

I appreciated that she thought about me. "Thanks."

"I really miss you, Cormac."

"Not as much as I miss you." My roommate for the night remained out, and I shut the drapes.

Coach had implemented the doubling, sometimes tripling up of single players to reduce unneeded wild nights. It didn't always work, but we'd seen a decent decline in hangovers and sleeplessness in the players. The buddy system kept players more focused on team goals rather than individual gratification.

Stol stayed at the bar—a good thing because I didn't want to shut down my call with Keelie. In fact, I wanted to see how far she'd let me go.

"I wish I could kiss you," I murmured. Just the idea made me hard.

"Mmm... I like your kisses."

I smiled. "I'd like to do more than just kiss you, Keelie."

"I...I'd like that, too." I liked her breathless, wanting me.

"Where should I kiss you?"

"I don't know..." she began.

"You're safe with me, sweet girl. Always."

"I...I've never..."

"And we don't have to do anything you don't want."

She turned quiet. My heart thudded against my ribs.

"My jawline. My neck. My breast." Keelie's voice grew throatier with each comment.

"I'd love to nuzzle and nip at your skin."

I slid my hand into my sweatpants, then under my boxer briefs. I gave my dick a pump. *Oh yeah, that feels good.* "I can't wait to see your nipples. Are they a soft pink? A light brown? Do they pout or get firm when you're aroused?"

"This conversation turned so hot," she gasped.

"Want me to stop?"

"N-no. I…I want to… I want you, Cormac," she breathed, her voice a whisper. "So much it scares me."

"I'm lying here thinking about you. I wish I could touch you. Love you like you deserve."

Her breathing grew raspier. "I'm going to touch myself."

My erection jerked, and I gave the base a squeeze. "*Yes.*"

"Are you… Will you touch yourself?"

"Already am." I slid my fist up and down my shaft, wishing *her* hand touched me. "Where do you want me to touch you next?"

"I want to feel you suck my nipples." Keelie moaned.

"Are you plucking them?"

"Yes."

"I'd nuzzle, then kiss before I sucked one into my mouth. You'd be a handful. I want your soft flesh in my hand, molded to my palm."

Her breath sped up, which made me think she'd increased the circles on her clit.

"Cormac!" she cried out.

"That's right, sweet girl. Call my name while you pleasure yourself. Are you wet?"

"Yesssss." Her moan turned long and lush.

My dick jerked, and I gritted my teeth. My head swam. "I'd work my way down your body… Lick your navel and then suck that sweet little clit between my lips—"

"Oh, oh, oh!"

I pumped harder and faster, erupting to Keelie's cries of pleasure. I pulled my hand from my pants. Slowly, my breathing returned to normal.

"That was...so hot." She sounded dazed.

"It was. I loved doing that with you."

"I want to be with you, Cormac," she said, her voice still sultry from her cries, but so sweet.

"I want that, too." I rose from the bed, wincing at the wetness on my belly and my hand.

"I can't wait to see you."

"Me neither. Now, I need to shower and change before Stol gets back."

"Oh, right. Of course. I'll see you soon."

"You can count on that," I said.

CHAPTER 21
Keelie

My phone rang the next afternoon as I exited the school building, rushing to get home before Cormac arrived at my place. I juggled my purse, keys, and tote to grab my phone. Glancing at the screen, I smiled as I answered. "Hey, Mare! What's up?"

"I just wanted to tell you I'm moving."

My stomach rolled. "Um… Okay. Is that why you didn't show up on Tuesday?"

"No, that's not why." Her voice iced.

I frowned. "So, do you need help packing? I could—"

"It's done, Keelie. I'm on the way to the airport."

I frowned, blinked, tried to right my world. "I don't understand."

She snorted. "You never did."

"What does that mean?"

"It means I'm pissed you took the hockey player from me."

"Took…? *Cormac*?"

"He was supposed to like me," she snapped. "But you had to do that cute I'm-such-a-sweetheart-so-giving-and-thoughtful act he seems to lap up."

With trembling hands, I opened the car door and settled on the edge of my cloth seat—just in time because my knees gave out. "Y-you're telling me that after years of friendship, you're leaving because you're *jealous*?"

"No. I'm leaving because I'm sick of your goody-two-shoes bullshit. Bye. Lose my number."

She clicked off. My vision tunneled, blackening at the edges. "Wh-what just happened?" I whispered. My mind raced back over the brief conversation, over the anger and vindictiveness in Marian's tone. I shook my head, not willing to believe she'd treat me like that. We'd known each other since I helped her find her lecture hall that first week on the University of Houston's campus.

Marian didn't make friends easily. She was prickly—difficult—but she'd always been loyal to me. We'd gotten along, mainly because I didn't mind her directing our activities. Not that I couldn't do so, but it was easier to follow her lead. Since my first date with Cormac, though, she'd been even more short-tempered. And now this was it? *We were finished*? Maybe I hadn't known Marian as well as I'd thought.

Clenching my jaw, I dragged myself into my car and started the engine. My hands continued to shake, but I drove to Marian's condo building.

"She's no longer a resident," explained Judd at the front desk. Pity filled his eyes as he cleared his throat. "And, ah, she said to tell you to…" He leaned closer and whispered, "*Eff off*, if you ever showed up."

I stared at him, mouth gaping nearly as wide as the wound in my heart. I blinked back tears. "She…she…did?"

Judd pressed his lips together, seeming unsure how to proceed. "Ms. Lindell wasn't popular with the residents or the staff."

I shook my head. This made little sense. Marian was my *friend*.

I didn't have many of those—and by intention because I'd learned not to trust from my parents. They'd been damn fine teachers.

"She was arrogant… Difficult," he added after a moment.

Understanding bloomed as I reconsidered my previous thoughts about the woman I'd long considered a friend. Apparently, her jealousy was stronger than her loyalty. Maybe I'd always been a means to an end for her. "You mean she was an entitled bitch who threw temper tantrums when she didn't get her way."

Judd raised his eyebrows and studied me for a long moment before he looked away. "She's no longer one of our residents because of a campaign by other condo owners who believed her attitude wasn't a good reflection on the building."

"Wow," I whispered. Sounded like *that* was why she'd moved. Nothing really to do with me. I pressed a hand to my stomach as I stared around the opulent lobby. How had I been so wrong about Marian? Why hadn't I seen her as others did?

I must have asked those questions aloud because Judd reached over and patted my shoulder twice. "If I may, Ms. Hayes, you're much better off without that, er, drama in your life."

I nodded and somehow made it back out to my car, my head a jumble. Judd's words looped through my mind as I drove home—to the house where Marian had bullied me into shaving the popcorn bits from my ceiling. Instead of helping me, she'd needed to "take a call," then grab a drink, and then use the restroom. She'd left me with the gallon of paint and a roller. *Shit.* I'd spent multiple hours on a ladder, alone, doing a project I hadn't wanted to take on, to appease a woman who'd never truly cared for me.

Once inside, I sat in my living room, staring up at my smooth ceiling. I did like it better. How it had gotten there... the hurt would lessen with time. I was used to being hurt, to being betrayed.

It seemed Marian was like my father—a liar, a manipulator. She'd used me, just like my father had used my mother. Not that my mother was a saint. She'd let me down too many times for me to remember, always chasing the next man who'd take care of her. I'd been an afterthought throughout my teen years, and my mother would never see me as anything other than the burden my father had dumped on her.

Maybe the problem here was me. If I couldn't trust my mother or a woman I'd known for years, it didn't seem wise to trust Cormac.

CHAPTER 22
Cormac

I knocked on Keelie's aluminum door, hearing the hollow reverberation inside. Anticipation sliced through me.

After our scorching phone sex, I'd been looking forward to touching her, kissing her. Loving her. Now, *finally*, I'd get my chance.

I heard her moving around inside, and then she opened the door. I'd planned to kiss her senseless, but one look at her swollen, bloodshot eyes, and all thoughts of seduction fled.

"What's wrong?"

"Nothing," she said, monotone. "I don't feel great, and I'm not interested in company right now. Thanks for stopping by."

She moved to shut the door, but I shoved my foot and hand forward, grasping the edge before it could fully close.

"Hey, you can talk to me," I coaxed.

"No, I can't." Her chin wobbled.

My heart ached. Keelie's sadness felt different from my many years with Shannon's tears. My ex had cried at commercials, if her nail polish smudged, if I returned home late, if I lost a game, if she was angry with me, if she lost an argument... I always thought that was weird because then she went into rhetoric—arguing—for a living. But she'd explained that she needed a chance to release the tension she carried from work. I'd secretly thought she manipulated me.

But Keelie was trying to kick me out, not get me to do something for her.

"Don't push me away," I implored. "I want to help."

She tipped her head back and met my gaze, her eyes filled with hurt. My breath caught.

"I'm not sure that's a good idea. You...you travel a lot. You won't be around if I have a problem, so I shouldn't lean on you."

Fear gripped me. *Not this.* "Yeah, I travel. Too often. I don't like that part. And you're right. I won't be here to hug you like this." I reached around the door and wrapped her in my arms. She melted against me in increments, her body shuddering as she finally nestled her cheek to my chest with a soft sigh.

I hated her grief but holding her like this felt right.

"But that doesn't mean I don't want to know what's going on with you," I continued. "Or that I don't care."

"You put your team first."

I dropped my cheek to the top of her head. "I didn't with Shannon, and that got me booted from Toronto. So then I spent five years focusing only on my team, and you know what?"

I waited until she asked, "What?"

"That wasn't the right choice either because I've been lonely. I've missed having someone to share with—the details of my day, a drink, a snuggle in bed."

She blinked up at me, mouth open just enough to show her teeth. One of her bottom ones sat a little in front of the other, and her top right incisor overlapped its neighbor just a hair. She wasn't perfect or perfected by veneers and personal trainers and Botox and surgeries. Keelie was a product of her life experiences—some of which haunted her.

"You…want to snuggle?" she said after a moment.

"The other night I loved it."

Her expression softened.

"Who doesn't like to touch another person?"

"Serial killers?"

I chuckled. "I'll give you that one. But who else wouldn't?"

She pursed her lips. "Grumpy buttholes who yell at you to get off their lawn?"

I shook my head. "Untrue. I think those guys want comfort and love more than most. That's why they're grumpy. Kind of like a beautiful woman I know who keeps trying to shut me out because something bad happened in her life." I tapped the tip of her nose. She scrunched it, and that was so cute. I had to press my lips to the crinkles.

She giggled as she pressed her nose into my chest. My world righted. I would break some body parts or threaten people or, hell, pay them off if it meant Keelie wouldn't cry. But this didn't feel like love—not like the emotion I'd had for Shannon. *This* was bigger and scarier because it was so uncontrollable.

She could hurt me. *Badly.* But as I looked down into those bloodshot eyes so filled with hope, yearning for the love denied her, I couldn't fathom me doing anything other than falling hard for Keelie Hayes.

"Ready to tell me what's bothering you?" I asked a little while later.

I'd maneuvered us to her couch—an uncomfortable but sleek design too short for me to stretch my legs out. Worse, the low back couldn't support my shoulders and neck. I squirmed, trying to find a position where parts of me weren't screaming in pain or stabbed with pins and needles.

"Marian left," Keelie said.

I stilled. My left hand cupped her shoulder, my right her hip. Keelie picked at my jeans, worrying a thread from the pattern. I'd end up with a hole, but I didn't ask her to stop. If that made her feel better, I'd wear holey jeans or buy another pair.

With a long sigh, Keelie recounted her phone conversation with Marian, and then the one with the concierge at Marian's building. I held her, trying to keep my muscles relaxed, but damn, that was hard. My jaw ticked as I clamped my teeth together.

"She doesn't sound like much of a friend."

"I agree," Keelie said. "But that blindsided me because I thought we were friends. Looking back now, I have a different lens—a clearer one, I hope. But this also shows me I'm not the best judge of character, and if I was wrong about Marian…" She trailed off, but the rest of the statement sprawled in front of me.

"Don't," I said, tone sharp.

She tensed. "Don't what?"

"Don't compare me to her. That's going to piss me off."

She looked up at me quickly. "I…I didn't… I wasn't…"

"You already did. That's why you tried to kick me out earlier." I extricated myself from her and rose so I could pace. "Is it always going to be like this? Me fighting to prove I won't leave?"

"I…I told you I have trust issues," she ground out.

"Yeah, but you haven't told me what those are."

She jutted her jaw and looked away. "I'm not ready."

"So maybe the problem isn't me being trustworthy. Maybe the problem is you being unwilling to trust."

"Exactly," she snapped. "I'm the *only* fool who didn't see what Marian really was. Which brings me right back to how would I even know if you were playing me?"

I turned back to look at her. "I've shared large parts of my life, my painful past with you. Those things aren't easy to talk about, but I trusted you with them. I'm not asking you to blurt out your entire history, but this—between us—means something. Right?"

Her lips quirked but her expression remained sad. "Yes. You promise you won't hurt me?"

I didn't know why she asked like that, but it seemed to come from a place of terrible hurt.

CHAPTER 23
Keelie

Cormac took my shoulders and brought me against his warm, hard chest. "I promise I'll never intentionally hurt you."

Hissing out a breath, I fought the urge to snuggle closer. I failed. "I…I'm terrible with arguments. During fights, I shut down."

"Thank you for telling me so I can understand you better." He nuzzled my temple. "I need something from you."

I worried over my stupidity in believing Cormac right now, even as he made me feel warm and safe. I shifted, uncomfortable with my need for answers, for reassurance, even as I battled my need to push him away. Wouldn't that be safer?

What if this wasn't what it seemed? He was a professional athlete. Those guys cheated on their spouses or girlfriends with regularity. Still, I closed my eyes and inhaled his scent. "All right."

"I need to know you'll talk to me." His voice garbled, as if he were swallowing some thick emotion.

I rested my cheek on his chest before I looked up and met his gaze. "Yes, I can see how that was hard for you. I'll try, Cormac."

"Good."

My lips curved a little, but I still felt lost. "I'm sorry I tried to push you away. I am. It's just…" I needed to give him some- thing—to prove I *was* trying. As I blurted, "My father cheated,"

I fisted my hands.

Not even half of the story, but I couldn't push any deeper into my past. Not now, anyway.

We settled back on my couch, and Slippers padded into the room. Never one for drama, she'd disappeared when voices rose. Now that our volume was normal, she leaped onto Cormac's lap and presented him with her back. He petted her in long strokes.

"I understand how much that can hurt."

Because Shannon cheated. We turned silent.

"I can't fix what I don't understand," he added after a moment.

Stricken, I tensed. "I see." *Please don't push me for more now. I'm trying…I'm really trying to share with you.*

He must have seen something in my expression because his softened. "I planned a date for us," he said.

I released some of my stress in my next breath. "You did? Golfing, right?"

"Well, that's tomorrow."

"Do you still want to go?" I asked carefully.

He nodded. "I do, and I think this is something we'll both enjoy."

"Okay," I whispered.

He smiled. "Good. Are you ready?"

"May I have five minutes?"

"Sure. Whatever you need."

I changed into a fresh outfit that made my butt look awesome and boosted my confidence as I considered how easygoing Cormac could be. His determination always simmered, but with me, he wasn't competitive. I appreciated the difference, especially after today's debacle. I shoved my feet into a pair of low-heeled sandals and grabbed my purse.

Excitement fizzed in my belly as I settled next to him in his SUV, face washed and mascara re-applied. "Where are we going?"

He glanced at me once he'd merged onto the highway. "Patience, little grasshopper."

I rummaged through my purse until I found my lip gloss, which I applied, smacking my lips to make sure the moisturizer went on evenly.

"You're so cute," he said.

"Um, okay."

"And distracting."

"That's not so good when you're driving," I said.

"Yeah, well, I can't help that I'm attracted to you."

"That's a biological response," I said.

He smirked. "I know."

I giggled. "No, I mean attraction is based on how my immune system smells to you and how yours smells to me. There's an organ behind the sinuses that filters for the right smell."

"That I didn't know. I've never heard that before." He put on his blinker and steered toward the off-ramp. "Are you messing with me?"

"No, I learned about it in a science video, but I thought maybe the guy made it up, so I read about it."

"That's interesting. So, my brain understands you're a good match for me based on some tiny chemicals—aren't those phero-mones? Those I have heard of."

I shrugged. "Kind of. But more complicated."

He tossed me that gorgeous smile that made my tummy flutter. "Not unlike a woman I know."

I shook my head. He wasn't wrong. I looked out the window and gasped. "Are we…"

"I asked you to golf with me, right?"

"Yes, but that's tomorrow."

"Well, this is step one. I understand this is one of the best courses in Houston. Considering it shares a name with our team, it seemed like the perfect choice."

I gaped as he pulled onto a narrower road with pristine grass on either side. The green shaded from pale to darker in neat rows, dotted by a few flags. I bounced in my seat as Cormac pulled into a parking spot near the front doors of the clubhouse. While the façade was like many other buildings in the area, the steeply-pitched roof reminded me of a French chateau. "I came here for a wedding a couple of years ago," I said as I tried to take in every inch of the perfect, emerald-green grass and shimmering blue ponds. "The space where they had their reception is giant with this beautiful wood-planked ceiling. I loved that space."

Cormac chuckled. "I can tell. We'll have to come back another time so you can show it to me, but tonight, we're here for a lesson."

I faced him, eyes bugging. "Y-you bought me a lesson with a golf pro?"

"I bought *us* a lesson with a golf pro. I've never played before, and I'm not going out there to embarrass myself tomorrow."

I flung myself across the console and wrapped my arms around his neck, not caring that the hard plastic in the center dug into my ribs. "This is the best date ever." I kissed him, trying to imbue all my thanks and happiness into the touch of lips.

He brushed my hair off my forehead and cheek. "I think I get why you shut down and pull away, but I want you to remember that I care about you, Keelie. A lot."

He waited patiently while I studied him. Finally, I nodded. "I understand. I care about you, too. A lot." And because the moment was getting heavy, I added, "More now because you got me a lesson with a golf pro!"

He laughed as he released me. Opening his door, intent on coming around to help me out, he frowned when I bounced out of my seat and met him at the hood.

After a shake of his head, he took my hand and led me toward the entrance.

He stopped just short of the door, and I turned to face him. He cleared his throat. "No ditching me for the golf dude, okay?"

My grin widened. Cormac did not know how amazing he was. He'd listened to my interests and read between the lines and found the most perfect gift for me—one I'd never give myself. Golf lessons were impractical when I needed to be aware of my budget. But this would increase my enjoyment of a game I already loved, in part because I'd play with him.

But he actually seemed nervous behind his poor attempt at a joke, so I rose on my tiptoes and kissed his dimpled chin. "Remember when I asked about being exclusive? I meant it."

Cormac released a gusty sigh. "Good. I want to keep it that way."

If he could make me this giddy, I imagined he'd never have to worry.

CHAPTER 24
Cormac

Keelie lifted and lowered her feet in their new golf spikes, wiggling her cute butt. I'd asked Denny, our teacher, to provide us each with the proper equipment, and Keelie now sported iridescent purple spikes and a matching visor. I'd chosen a much more sedate gray version. When she protested about me buying her a set of clubs, too, I nipped her ear as I whispered, "You need the right equipment if you want to win."

She shivered and tipped her head back to meet my gaze. "You think you're going to beat me, hockey man?"

I enjoyed her brand of teasing, wanted more of it. Maybe she wasn't the only one who needed reassurances. "I have no clue," I told her. "But it'll be fun to see how it goes tomorrow."

I meant that. I'd never played before, but I wanted to do this with her...for her. So, I paid attention to Denny's instructions, awed by the ease with which Keelie absorbed his suggestions into her stance and swing. Her affinity for golf reminded me of mine for hockey—she was a natural. I was not.

And yet, here I was. Keelie's round ass kept distracting me as I lined up my shot. I took a deep breath, striving to find my focus. She wiggled again. But this time I caught her grin before she looked back toward the driving range.

"You're doing that on purpose," I called.

"What?" She looked over her shoulder at me, all wide-eyed innocence.

After finally managing my shot—which landed far short of its intended target. I leaned on my new club. Golf was...okay. I kind of sucked at it, but I could understand the allure of being outside, moving your body, and competing. But I enjoyed winning, and ass distraction aside, Keelie had an aptitude for the game that I lacked. After coaching her for ten minutes, Denny had said, "Her understanding of the game is innate and spot-on."

Keelie prepared for her shot, and with a graceful backswing, lifting the club just as Denny showed her, she powered through with her hips, slamming the driver against the ball in the sweet spot. The ball curved up and out in an elegant parabola, landing a good three hundred feet on the driving range.

Keelie bounced and leaped into my arms, wrapping her legs around me and peppering my face with kisses. "I love this date."

I clasped her thighs in my hands, tugging her against me as I caught her lips and deepened the kiss. She tasted sweet with just a hint of heat, and she gave me everything. Keelie had two modes: cautious and all-in.

"Want to get dinner?" I asked, pulling back just enough to articulate my words.

"If that's what you want," she replied, her eyes heavy with desire.

CHAPTER 25
Keelie

Cormac took my hand but had to let go to grab the bag with his clubs, then mine. He'd bought me an entire set of golf clubs. And shoes. He bowled me over with his generosity.

"Oh, let me take those." I hurried forward and clasped the shoulder strap of my bag. He arched a brow as if to say, *I got this*, but I didn't want anyone touching my beauties…even if Cormac had handled their purchase. I slid the bag onto my shoulder and clasped his hand in mine. "This was so much fun. Thank you."

Cormac led me through the air-conditioned clubhouse where we found Denny to say goodbye.

"Be sure to let me know who wins tomorrow," he said with a smile. "My money's on you, Keelie."

I laughed, shaking my head. "It's going to be fun, no matter the outcome."

Denny shared a look with Cormac, who shrugged. "She's not competitive."

Denny, tapping his chin with his forefinger and middle finger, nodded. Then he sighed. "Such talent. Still, I hope you have a great time."

I trotted behind Cormac, frowning as I tried to untangle the guys' conversation. "What did that mean?"

Cormac opened the back of his SUV and slid his clubs into

the car. It took me another moment to relinquish mine. Part of
me wanted to take the putter into the front seat with me so I
could snuggle it.

"What were you talking about?" I asked again.

Cormac opened the door. I slid into the seat. He leaned his
body against the edge of the frame.

"You're very good. With practice, you might be LPGA good."

I laughed—until I realized Cormac wasn't even smiling. He
continued to study me as if I mystified him. "I don't think you
understand how rare you are, pretty girl."

I tucked an errant strand of hair behind my ear. "I'm just me,
Cormac. That's all."

He smiled, and his eyes filled with heat as he leaned closer and
kissed me. His mouth, hot sin, made me shudder with need. I
clenched my thighs, the barrage of latent passion slamming into
me, rolling over me, putting me under Cormac's spell.

He groaned as he ended the kiss, his features tightening with
lust. "The more I get to know about you, Keelie Hayes, the more
I want you."

Cormac drove while I tried to regulate my heart rate…and my
raging need. For him.

"Where are we going?" I asked.

"My house."

"Do you think that's a good idea?"

He shot me a side-eye. "I think it's a great idea. But you have
to know I won't pressure you."

The provocative look accompanying that statement made my

thighs clench even tighter, and the pulsing between them grow stronger.

"Don't worry, Keelie. I'm old enough to understand that us acting on that desire has consequences."

At my flinch, he patted my hand.

"Consequences don't have to be bad. It could mean we're both post-orgasmic and relaxed." He winked.

I licked my lips. "You were married, Cormac. That's baggage." I paused. "Especially the way yours ended."

He pulled into his driveway, slowing so the gate could slide open. His jaw ticked, and his eyes were darker than normal. "Fair enough. But you won't explain your baggage, and it's pissing me off."

I reached over and clasped his hand in both of mine. "Fair enough," I said, tugging a reluctant smile from his lips. "It stems from my parents' relationship." I heaved a sigh. "I know I struggle with trust after I saw how devastated my mother was when my father…" I licked my lips. My heart pounded in my chest, and I chickened out, going instead with the only comment I'd ever made about my parents' failed marriage. "When my father cheated."

I stared down at my hands for a moment before I peeked over at Cormac from under my lashes. "And I don't like feeling lesser than your ex."

He shot me a horrified look. "Ah, Keelie. No. That's not true."

I shrugged. "It's how I feel. She's a lawyer. Smart, stylish, beautiful."

"She didn't understand that love means sacrifice. Plus, you're all those things."

He blew out a breath, focused on overcoming my inadequacies. They weren't fun to discuss either, but at least he'd dropped my trust issues…for now.

"I wish you could know how much I want you." He pulled through the gate and slanted a look in my direction. "On second thought, no I don't. My thoughts might scare you."

A thrill worked its way across my lower belly. "Because your thoughts are…"

He considered me for a long moment. "Us—hot, sweaty, naked."

CHAPTER 26
Keelie

After Cormac's comments about us sweaty and naked, when we went inside he prepared dinner. I went to the cabinets he'd pointed out to me before to collect plates and glasses. Once I set them on the table, I wiped my palms on my thighs.

"I thought you wanted to be sweaty and naked," I blurted.

His lips curled upward in a smile as he stirred the pot. Steam wafted around him, making the edges of his light-brown hair curl.

"Oh, I do. But…" He moved toward me, large and graceful. His understated confidence was intrinsic. Heat pooled in my belly. He caged me between his arms, his hands flat on the counter behind me. Leaning down, he nuzzled into my hair. "You're not ready yet, and I will not push you."

Push! Please. I bit my lip, wondering where that thought had come from. Well, I knew where: my body *craved* him. But my mind wasn't there yet.

That he realized that—that he reined in his desire instead of trying to seduce me—made me melt against him.

Maybe…maybe I could trust him?

He kissed my temple even as he drew back. "Dinner's ready."

I gulped, trying to regain my equilibrium. Once we'd settled at his table, hunger hit hard, and I draped my napkin in my lap, ready to dig in.

Our conversation flowed. Cormac liked big dogs but had never had one. He was a loyal friend and teammate—no surprise there—and he hated jalapeños.

"Must make it hard with all the Tex-Mex 'round here."

He shot me a sardonic look as he finished eating his shrimp and creamed spinach.

"So, what's your schedule tomorrow?" I asked.

"I have to be at practice by eight, but I'll be back before one, for lunch—unless you want to come with me to the rink?"

I smiled, warmed that he'd offered. "That's allowed?"

"Sure. Coach's wife and daughter attend when they can, and various staff are in the stands. Sometimes the CATS come, too."

"I'd love to see you practice."

He'd piled my plate with more than twice my typical serving. And while I'd tucked in, there was no way I could finish. I pushed the dish away, trying to be dainty when I wiped my lips.

He grabbed my plate along with the dishes and moved back into the kitchen, shaking his head when I offered to help. "I like things a certain way," he said, his expression adorably sheepish.

I nodded and watched as he rinsed and loaded the dishwasher, lining up the glasses and plates, and placing the forks and spoons pointed upward in the silverware slots, but the knives down. He wiped his counters, then wiped out his sink before taking the cloth to the laundry room. He returned, stifling a yawn.

"I can call an Uber," I said.

Cormac shook his head. "I'll drive you."

I pressed a hand to his chest. "I can't let you do that. You're tired, and you need your rest."

He took my hand, lifting it to kiss my palm. Shivering, I admitted to myself that I liked his lips on me. I liked that he hugged me, kissed me; those actions made me feel desirable. Needed.

"I don't want to argue with you," he said, yawning again. "Sorry. I guess the golf practice did me in." He tilted his head, considering me. "You could stay here…since you're already planning to come to practice with me tomorrow." He winked. "We'd be saving on gas, protecting the environment."

"I have nothing to wear—"

"You can sleep in one of my T-shirts, and we can wash your clothes. Or you can wear that cute little golf shirt and shorts we picked up today."

He continued to break through my barriers, not letting me put up a fight to keep him out…because I didn't want to keep him out. Not really.

"What about Slippers?"

Cormac pursed his lips. "She ate already tonight, right?" At my nod, he continued. "We'll get up a bit earlier tomorrow so we can swing by your place to feed her on the way to the arena."

"Okay," I said.

Smiling, he took my hand, keeping the clasp light, and tugged me out of the kitchen. He checked the front door and slider before leading me up the stairs.

"Let's get your night attire sorted. You want to stay with me—that's my preference—or in a guest room?"

The heat built between my legs again. "I'd like to stay with you."

On the landing, he turned to face me, clasping my face between his palms. "Ah, Keelie. Being with you makes me happy." His lips quirked, and his eyes shone. "Keep telling you, I want you. Here with me. In bed with me. At my practices. At my games."

My heart rate revved, and I leaned forward, but Cormac wheeled around, taking my hand again as he led me into his bedroom. He popped into the bathroom for a moment and then emerged. "There's a new toothbrush on the counter. I'll grab that shirt for you. Do your thing."

I closed the heavy wooden door behind me and groaned. Cormac had tunneled under my defenses. I wanted him. Most women in the city—hell, probably the world—wanted him. He was beautiful, but more importantly, he was thoughtful. And he could kiss.

Yet still I remained leery, worried about a future I couldn't predict. Stability was the paramount need in my life, and Cormac might not offer that. I couldn't go back to the uncertainty of my childhood.

Bottom line? Cormac could break my heart—the one I'd never gotten back together right after my father left.

CHAPTER 27
Cormac

Keelie had turned quiet last night, though I tried to ease her concerns about me just wanting her there for sex. I wanted sex—oh, man did I desire orgasms—but I craved her in my bed, snuggled close to me, more. So I refused to push her.

Holding her through the night relaxed me, her breath light as it skated over my skin, and I slept hard. I woke to my alarm, feeling happy as opposed to disgruntled. I eased from the bed, and after a quick trip to the bathroom, I headed downstairs to make coffee.

I rummaged in the kitchen and took care of a few things. A few minutes later, I heard the water running and smiled. Keelie cared about punctuality, her sense of responsibility was deeply ingrained. When she entered the kitchen, I admired her high ponytail and the golf shirt she'd chosen yesterday. It was form-fitting and lavender—not a color I'd have chosen, but it looked great on her. She also wore the coordinating capri pants...and cotton panties with pink polka dots I'd washed for her last night and run up to her this morning once they dried. Yeah, I'd be thinking about those little dots all day.

Her sun visor dangled from her fingers. I handed her a cup of coffee as I pressed a kiss to her temple. "Morning, pretty girl."

"It is." She smiled as she turned and swiped her mouth against mine. She rubbed her thumb on my lip to remove her lip gloss. "Did you sleep well?"

"I did. You?"

"Yeah." She seemed surprised. "And I'm looking forward to watching you skate." Her smile bloomed, making my chest ache with joy. "Then, golf!"

I chuckled as I tapped her nose. "Want some of my smoothie?"

She wrinkled her nose, shaking her head.

"Well, drink your coffee, and we'll go."

"Should we take water?"

I showed her where I kept my reusable bottles, then went back upstairs to change into my gym gear.

When I returned, she'd stuffed her large purse with water bottles and the trail mix my trainer made for me. I added a couple of bananas to her stash, and we walked out the backdoor and settled into my vehicle.

I smiled over at her, glad to see her joy and curiosity back in full bloom.

~

"Who's the chick, and why's she here?" Naese asked.

"Because I brought her."

Naese held up his hands, making me aware of my aggressive stance. "Cool, dude. Just…didn't know. She's pretty."

"She is." I clenched my fist inside my glove. "And I want to make a sexist-as-fuck remark about her being *mine*, but that shit isn't cool."

Naese chuckled. "Got it, Cap. I won't hit on the new hot chick."

Adam, our goalkeeper, patted my shoulder. "It's okay to claim your woman." He took a long slug of water.

I shrugged, squinting. "She's her own person."

"I hear you, and Naomi would throw a fit if she heard this convo, but…Naomi's still mine. I put a ring on that finger and promised forever, same as she did, which makes me hers." He winked. "When it's mutual, it's *all* good."

"Well, Keelie and I are new, and I haven't dated in twenty years, so I don't want to mess this up. Do you think Naomi would keep Keelie company at the game tomorrow?"

"I couldn't stop her," Adam said. "That woman is a menace." His smile turned indulgent. He loved his wife, and I couldn't help but be envious—because he knew she felt the same.

"Great. Mind if I text her? Just to make sure."

"Go for it, man." Adam tossed his water bottle to a staff member, pulled on his gloves, picked up his stick, and skated to his goal.

"Why's your girl dressed like a frat boy?" Maxim asked.

Naese snickered. I shot Maxim an angry look. "Because I'm taking her to play golf after this."

Maxim's face crinkled into a confused expression. "Golf? Why?"

"Because she likes it, she's good at it, and she's excited to kick my ass."

Maxim tipped his head. "Fair."

"What happened with the girl you met last night?" Nik asked. "She had a double name."

"Ida Jane." Maxim scowled.

"You met a woman?" I asked.

"We went to a restaurant, and some guy accosted a woman out front," Maxim growled.

"Not quite," Nik said, smiling. "She gave him hell. Knocked him on his ass—which he deserved."

Maxim shrugged, but I noted the dull red creeping up his neck and under his scruff. "I like her."

I clapped him on the shoulder. "Hope that works out."

He grunted.

"You get her number?" Nik asked.

"Yeah. I got it." Maxim scowled. "But I'm not sure I'm going to call her."

Naese leaned in close to me. "He's already texting her." He darted off when Maxim lunged for him, leaving Nik and me chuckling.

"You're golfing later?" Coach asked from behind me. He must have been leaning against the boards. His clipboard sat beneath his forearms. "I said hi to your lady." He tipped his head toward Keelie, who sat engrossed in her phone.

"That's the plan," I said.

"Paloma likes to play."

"Cool."

"Where are you going?" Coach asked.

"Wildcat."

He nodded. "Let's finish this."

Once practice ended, I skated over to Keelie, who was chatting with Maxim and Nik. I enjoyed seeing her so relaxed around my friends.

"Yeah, give us a bit to clean up and grab something to eat, then we'll meet you there," Nik said.

"Meet who where?" I asked.

Maxim smiled. "Coach set up tee times for those of us interested in a golf afternoon. You know, team building."

I groaned. "No, this is my date with Keelie."

Maxim slapped my shoulder. "And a bunch of the guys."

I cursed, anger bubbling. Keelie giggled. I shot her a sour look. "What?"

"I think it's cute that you guys like to do things together."

I shrugged. "Until I want to do things with just you."

"Golf isn't a just-you thing," Nik said, his expression serious. "That's sex."

"Dude, chicks don't like that talk," Maxim muttered.

"They don't like being called chicks either," Keelie replied.

To my surprise, she leaned over the boards and kissed me. My lips tingled, but I wanted more. That was going to be a constant issue with Keelie.

"See you in a few—with your buddies—for our golf date," she said with a wave.

CHAPTER 28
Keelie

Cormac's frustration was adorable. I understood why he felt that way, but I also appreciated the opportunity to get to know more about him—and his friends. I figured after being blinded by Marian's duplicity, I needed to do all the research into Cormac I could. How he interacted with the people closest to him should give me a better sign of his true personality.

He grumbled on our way to the course, but when he saw a tall redhead with knockout curves waiting just inside the door of the clubhouse, he strode over and wrapped her in a hug. I hung back, unsure who this woman was or how to proceed.

"Good to see you, Cormac," she said. "Who's this?"

He stepped back and took my hand, beaming as he introduced me. "Keelie Hayes, occupational therapist and golf pro, meet Paloma Whittaker, mom extraordinaire and Wildcatters chief wrangler."

Paloma laughed, but she also grinned broader. Cormac did that to people—he noted what put them at ease or made them happy.

"I'm married to Silas, the coach," she said. "Cormac left out that detail. I hope you're not too angry with Silas for stealing your time alone." Her expression turned earnest. "I don't want to cause problems between any of you."

Cormac ran his palm up the back of his neck and shot me a

glance. "It's okay."

Paloma raised an eyebrow behind the turquoise frames of her glasses. "Mmm… I see how this went down." She lifted sunglasses from the V of her T-shirt and perched them on her nose. She patted Cormac's cheek before she strode toward a man outside, who pulled a fourth golf cart into a line out front.

"What's that about?" I asked.

"Don't know. Let's get our gear settled, okay? You hungry?" Cormac asked.

"No. I'm good. The trail mix hit the spot."

He'd eaten the bulk of it, along with both bananas and another smoothie he'd made at the arena.

We went back outside, where the golf cart man was now deep in conversation with Paloma. After a moment, he turned toward Cormac and me and waved toward the first golf cart. "You can tee off on the first hole whenever you're ready." He smiled politely.

Cormac glanced back at Paloma, who waved us on. "Want to drive?" he asked.

A thrill went through me, followed by a flash of anxiety. "No. I'm a little afraid of falling into the pond."

He chuckled as he stowed our clubs. I settled into the passenger seat, and he got behind the wheel. We pulled out just as the rest of the team trooped up to the clubhouse.

"We have ten minutes until our tee time, so if you want a drink, go in and grab one," Paloma told them as we passed.

I glanced back at the group of large men milling around.

"Why are they heading out now?" Naese asked, motioning toward us.

"Because this was Cormac's idea for his girlfriend, and we're all party crashers," Paloma said, her tone as no-nonsense as any teacher I'd had the pleasure of working with at school.

I giggled as the player slunk into the building, properly cowed. "I like her," I said.

Cormac nodded. "Good. She's been an important part of the team for years. Keeps us in line."

"That's why I like her."

Cormac stopped the cart at the designated spot, and I slid on my golf glove and pulled out my tee, ball, and club.

"Want to hit first?" I asked.

He shook his head.

"All chivalry?"

He grinned, his teeth white against the shadow of his visor. "Nope. I'm still taking notes on your form."

I winked as I sashayed past him. I settled my ball, then looked down the fairway. Once I widened into my stance, I swung back and forward. The club hit the ball just like Denny had taught me, and it sailed down the green in a smooth parabola.

Cormac whistled. "Hella shot, pretty girl."

I grinned, pleased as the ball rolled to within fifty yards of the pin, even as I pulled my tee and moved out of Cormac's way. He frowned, lips pursed in concentration as he drew his club back and hit the ball.

He grunted as his ball rolled to a stop about thirty feet to the left of mine—at the edge of a sand trap.

Cormac's athleticism showed itself throughout the eighteen holes.

He had more power and stamina than I did, but I had a good feel for the sport.

"That's the game," I said as he tapped in his final putt. I handed him the scorecard, and he added up his total.

"Seven over par for me," he said. "Par for you."

"Women's par for me. That's different."

"You're a woman, so you get par. You beat me by seven strokes."

"That's not exactly true—"

He tugged me close, ignoring how our visors hit, and kissed me.

"Tongue her later. I want to finish my game," Naese yelled as Maxim careened the cart toward us. I grinned into the kiss, but Cormac grumbled.

"Show some respect to the lady," he called.

"Oh, right. Please tongue her later—ow!"

Naese rubbed the back of his head, glaring at Maxim. Cruz laughed from his seat in the back.

"Cruz quit playing after the third hole," Nik reported. "He complained about blisters."

"Can't have those for our game tomorrow," Cruz said, unperturbed. He picked up a bottle of iced tea and took a long swig.

"I'm going to take my putt," Maxim said.

"You're in the fucking sand trap again," Nik pointed out. "Let me go so I can clear the green."

"You're not on the green," Maxim said. "You're still a hundred yards back there." He pointed behind him.

"Well, I'm doing better than Naese, who lost…how many balls was it—a dozen?—to the water."

"Golf's fucking hard," Naese grumbled.

"Not for Keelie," Cormac said, puffing with pride. "She played par for the course."

Maxim's scowl deepened. Cruz belly laughed, and Nik shot the middle finger as he hiked back down the green. Giggling, I leaned against Cormac.

None of this group fared as well as Cormac had, and the next foursome included Coach Whitaker, Paloma, Adam, and Luka. Coach and Paloma knew how to play, but as Paloma said, neither of them was very competent.

"I just like to be outside," she said. "Well, that and I can occasionally beat Silas." She winked. "He's still as competitive as his players. They put together a pot at the beginning. Don't worry, I covered the twenty bucks for each of you—least I could do after Silas commandeered your time together."

"What does that mean?" I asked.

Cormac tucked a strand of my hair behind my ear. "Whoever's got the lowest score wins the pot."

"Ah."

We moved to our cart, and I reached over to grab my water bottle just as Silas cursed. Looking up, I noted that he'd missed his putt, and the ball was now thirty feet to the other side. He strode over, glaring at the ball, and settled into his stance.

"He's going to pull it left," I muttered.

When he did, Cormac chuckled. "I don't know how you know that, but I love that you do."

"Why's that?" I adjusted my visor, wiping sweat from my brow.

"Because you're going to win the pot."

Flutters built in my belly, and I placed my hand there. "I can't. I didn't even put in money…"

"You will," Cormac said, confidence radiating from him. "None of us is as good as you."

Silas completed his round just as the last cart bumped along the path toward us. Cormac shot me a told-you-so glance before he drove us back to the clubhouse. When we arrived, the guys returned their borrowed clubs, and the staff brought glasses of icy, cold water.

As we sipped, Paloma sidled up next to me, steering me toward an out-of-the-way spot near a wall. "They'll need to take some photos, probably sign some merch," she explained. On cue, the manager and more staff flooded the room, requesting photos and autographs.

She took another drink of her water before bringing the glass to her sun-warmed cheek. "Houston is hot, even during February."

"I don't know anything else," I said.

Paloma smiled. "I didn't either, before I met Silas."

"Is it hard?" I asked, turning toward her. "Being married to a celebrity."

Her smile shifted, becoming more indulgent. "Luckily, Silas isn't a genuine celebrity—not like a movie or rock star. So we can go places and never be bothered. But here, in this city, where people are used to seeing him… It's part of the job, I guess. And he loves what he does, so he doesn't complain about meeting fans' expectations."

I nodded. "I've never been asked for anything before—except

to change my treatment plan for a kid once. His parents didn't want him to be disabled. And he wasn't, just slower with development, which improved more rapidly after I got the interventions he needed in place."

Paloma gave me her full attention. "I like that you stuck to your guns, did what was best for the child, despite the outside pressure."

I fisted and opened my hands, trying to release some of the tension that had flowed into my body with the gathering crowd. "That's my job."

"Not everyone would maintain that position." She smiled, her eyes bright behind her glasses. "I like you, Keelie. I've seen a lot of women, too many women, parade through this organization over the last few years—not with Cormac," she hastened to say, no doubt in response to my stricken expression. "He's never dated. At least as far as I know. But the other boys…" She pursed her lips, clarifying that she didn't consider all the large men in front of her fully developed.

"I've always thought Cormac was special," she added after a moment. "And I think with the team captain showing these boys what they should look for in a partner, there's bound to be positive change. Just more slowly than I'd like."

I turned back to the crowd and found Cormac's attention on me. He'd been monitoring me, even surrounded by the rest of the team and ever-more fans. Pleasure spread through my chest. He was a good man—a very good one, just as Paloma had said. While daunted at the prospect of being the captain's partner, I liked the idea, too.

Marian had been wrong. I straightened my spine and squared

my shoulders. Cormac wanted *me*, needed me, and I *deserved* him. I knew he wanted more from me—all of me—and I wanted to give that to him.

As soon as we could get away from the craziness of Houston hockey fans.

CHAPTER 29
Cormac

"Thank you for today," Keelie said as we entered my house, Keelie carrying Slippers. We'd detoured by her place to collect her cat and all of its paraphernalia. I'd wrinkled my nose at the litter box, deciding to get one for my place, stat.

Keelie's nose, cheeks, and chin were pink from the sun, and her eyes sparkled with excitement. I left the litter box in the laundry room while Keelie carried the cat into the kitchen. Once Keelie set Slippers down, we watched her sniff the space before wandering off.

Keelie raised her gaze to me, and I aligned our hips and wrapped my arms around her waist before I kissed her. Her sweet taste bloomed across my tongue, and I craved more. Her fingernails dug into my shoulders as she opened her mouth. We both groaned as our tongues tangled, danced. Breathless, I moved down to inhale and nibble on her neck. She tipped her head back, pressing her breasts into my chest.

I tightened my arms, laving my tongue down the column of her throat. She slid one hand down my back to cup my butt. I pressed my groin against her as I teased the spot where her neck and shoulder met. Keelie crawled up my legs to wrap her thighs around my waist. The heat of her center rubbed against my aching dick. She shifted, searching for friction.

I gripped the kitchen counter behind her just in case my knees gave out. Damn, I wanted this woman. Lust swirled hot as I sought her lips again and settled her on the counter.

Before I asked, she'd tugged off her shirt and unclasped her bra. I palmed her soft breasts, loving how they plumped in my hands. I pinched her nipples between my thumbs and forefingers even as I sucked on her lower lip.

She reared back, expression tight. "Take off your shirt."

I whipped it off. She pressed her palms to my pecs, and I couldn't stop myself from flexing. She cooed over my muscles, petting me, and I panted even as I returned the favor.

"Let's go upstairs," she said.

She wrapped her arms and legs around me, and I slid an arm underneath that sexy ass before I stumbled toward the stairs. I felt drunk with need. Keelie torched my senses, and I struggled against my desire to tug down our pants right there in the hall. I maneuvered up the stairs and into my bedroom, dropping a knee onto the bed so she landed on the duvet. Before she could move, I'd divested her of her shoes and rested my hands on the waist-band of her pants.

"Can I…"

Her hands moved over mine and undid the button. I released her zipper. She lifted her hips as I slid the material down her legs.

And, just like that, my fantasy lay spread out before me: Keelie Hayes with her hair like a bright halo around her head, wearing those tiny, polka-dotted panties, lying on my bed.

"Fuuuuuuuck."

She lifted onto her elbows, causing her taut stomach muscles to flex. I tightened my abs, expecting her to touch me. Instead, she stripped off her panties and spread her legs just enough to give me a view of the treasure I wanted between them.

CHAPTER 30
Keelie

Trembling with nerves, I refused to let that stop me. I wanted this man, physically and emotionally…as close to me as possible. I wanted us to find happiness together. But my words failed me, and my tongue felt heavy in my mouth as he stared down at me.

Finally, he brought a large hand to my lower abdomen, just above my trimmed mound.

My muscles flexed and my legs shifted, restless.

His eyes were dark, his pupils wide, lips parted. His chest rose and fell in rapid pants. "You are so beautiful."

His voice, a soft rasp, rippled over my skin. I tipped my hips a little, arching into his hand. He groaned as he slid his hands to my thighs, then around to the back, before he tugged my legs open wider and yanked me to the edge of the bed. Dropping to his knees, he started kissing down the inside of my thigh. He nuzzled into my damp curls before he moved to the other side and started again. My breathing hitched and my hips shifted, restless, so damn needy. I stared up at the ceiling, trying to process all the feelings…. And then he licked me.

Right there. Where I needed him most. My hips shot off the mattress, and he chuckled. The decadent sound slid over my sensitized skin, pulling up gooseflesh and budding my nipples into hard peaks. He swirled his tongue around my clit and I screamed, slamming my foot into the bedding.

He licked me again, from my clit back, and then up again. My fingers dug into the soft silk of the comforter and twisted. I wasn't sure how much I could take, but I never wanted him to stop. He dipped his tongue inside me, tasting my lower lips as he had the ones I now bit to hold in the moans of pleasure straining my throat.

"Let me hear you, Keelie. Tell me what gives you pleasure."

"You…" My voice was so breathy. "Licking me. My clit." That was all I could get out because he suckled my little bud into his mouth, drawing it deep. I arched my neck, my back, pressing tighter to him, desperate for more pleasure even as I shocked myself with my reaction. I felt as if I were afire, the all-consuming ecstasy making me mindless to anything but more.

I panted even as I forced my arms to support me. I needed to see Cormac, there, between my legs. He slid a finger inside me. I moaned long and low. He smiled against my clit as he pumped the finger in and out. When he found the spot inside, he curled his finger against it, and I gripped my toes against his shoulders, using his position to leverage myself against his mouth. He slipped a second finger inside me, stretching me while he licked my nub.

The orgasm slammed over me, stealing my breath, sending me tumbling into bliss. I clenched and shook as I screamed his name. The sensations flowed over me, drawn out by his skillful fingers and tongue.

Eventually, the orgasm subsided, and I slid boneless to the bed, wrung out by the pleasure he'd provided. I felt his fingers in my hair, his lips against my neck, his nose nuzzling my cheek. My vision remained a little unfocused, but one thought remained: Cormac needed the same level of ecstasy I'd just experienced.

CHAPTER 31
Cormac

Keelie's wide eyes were dazed, her pink lips parted, her skin flushed from the pleasure I'd given her. She turned her head and smiled. It dazzled me. Maybe that's how I ended up on my back with Keelie's sweet butt cheeks pressed against my aching cock. The organ pulsed against my shorts, desperate to get inside her.

She slid her breasts against my chest as she pushed herself forward to rest against me. "That was amazing, Cormac. Truly."

Vulnerability flashed across her face, and I cupped the back of her head. She kissed me, and I groaned into her sweet mouth. Quick as a summer breeze, she darted off and removed my shoes, shorts, and underwear.

"I have condoms in the bedside drawer," I told her. "Let me get them."

"I'll get them," she said. She opened the drawer, stopped, and then frowned.

At that moment, I remembered the picture in there—one of me with Shannon from high school graduation. I cursed myself for that oversight because, as I watched, the sexy goddess Keelie pulled back, shrinking into herself. I mourned her loss.

"Keelie—"

She pulled out the condoms and turned to face me, eyes bright, a smile plastered on her face. "New box." She shook it.

"Keelie, I'm sorry. It's not what you think—"

She raised her eyebrows even as she edged away from me. "Mmm?"

I rose from the bed, reached around her, and grabbed the photo, throwing it out into the hall. Then, before she realized my intent, I snagged her around the waist and lifted her into my lap. My dick still ached, but my chest hurt more, especially while she remained stiff in my arms.

"Trust is hard for me." She'd told me that, and we'd just taken a huge, huge step backward—away from her learning she could trust me.

"Oh, my pretty girl, I'm sorry." I rocked her, petting her hair. "I'm sorry you're hurting."

She struggled against me, and I released her, though it took everything in me to let her go. Defiance flashed across her features as she tossed her head. "I thought you wanted to sex me up, Cormac."

"I did." Looking down at my rock-hard erection, I sighed. "I do. But I won't. I can't. Not with you thinking…whatever you're thinking."

She remained quiet, standing before me, an arm shielding her perky pink nipples. "You have a picture of your ex-wife in your bedroom, in your nightstand."

The accusation hung in the air between us.

CHAPTER 32
Keelie

Much as I wanted to snatch up my clothes and dress, it seemed ridiculous. Cormac had seen me nude. He'd just brought me to the best orgasm of my life.

Tears formed, but I refused to let them fall. His tortured expression kept me rooted to the spot, somehow unable to scramble away, to put the distance I needed between us. *Put on your clothes. Leave.*

He came toward me and touched my hair, his big hand tentative. He tucked the strand back, fingering the ends. "I'm sorry. I didn't realize that photo was there." He rubbed his hand over his cheek, darkened by the start of a five-o'clock shadow. He pulled me closer and lifted the covers on the bed, seeming to know I needed some shield for this conversation.

"Why?" I asked. I dropped the box of condoms—my eyes widened at the size, magnums—and scrambled underneath the sheet, tugging it up to my chest. I clenched the edge, my knuckles popping with the strain.

His expression turned even more mournful, but he didn't object. "My mother set it on my nightstand the only time she's visited. She doesn't believe in divorce. She thinks Shannon and I are perfect together. I tossed it in the drawer because I didn't want it out." His expression hardened.

We sat in silence.

"Um, this is awkward. I mean, the mood tanked, but we're still naked…" I said.

He laughed, and then so did I. Some of the tension eased. Finally, he sobered and turned toward me. He cupped my cheeks as he studied me, looking deep into my soul. "I'm sorry. I'd never hurt you, Keelie. Please, please, believe that."

I took my time searching his eyes. They were filled with my pain. "Okay."

He blew out a breath. "Want some dinner?"

"Um…" I looked down at his lap. Disappointment raced through me when I noted he was no longer hard. Not that I could have sex with him right now. I didn't trust him. I didn't trust anyone.

Hell, the woman I'd considered my best friend had used me. I lifted my knees and rested my cheek against them as I wrapped my arms around my shins. Confusion buffeted me.

Cormac kissed the top of my head before he rose from the bed and stretched. I enjoyed the play of muscles as they rippled over his sublime back. I pressed my legs together as a faint pulse throbbed in my core. *Not the time.*

Anger and jealousy whipped through me. Was what he'd told me true? Did he still have feelings for his ex? He'd said he didn't. My confusion grew into a storm, swirling in my chest. I didn't know what to do—how to fix this.

He turned toward me, his expression both amused and bleak. "Well, that didn't go according to plan. But that doesn't mean I don't want to spend time with you."

"Maybe I should go…"

He nodded. "If you want to, I understand. But I don't want you to leave." He settled next to me on the edge of the bed once more, close enough to touch, but he didn't try.

I licked my lips. "I don't know what to do, what to think…"

"Hey, this is new for me, too, Keelie. I'm trying. Putting myself out there after Shannon shattered me? It's fucking hard." His Adam's apple dipped, and his jaw clenched. "I never expected to meet someone again. Someone I could share my life with."

I tilted my head. "Are you saying you're thinking long-term between us?"

A smile flitted across his mouth. "Yeah. That's what I'm saying." His brows puckered. "I wasn't looking for anything, but then you happened." His expression softened and caring shone from his eyes. "I don't want to fight against us. I want to fight for us. For a future."

"I… It's fast…" I whispered.

"It is, but it isn't, really. You meeting the team solidified it for me. That's why I more than happy to take you by your place to pick up your cat and whatever you need—clothes, toiletries. I want you here. I'm *happier* with you here."

My heart fluttered and dipped, my confusion giving way to a burgeoning joy. But I tempered it with the ruthlessness I'd learned as a young girl. *Men say things. They don't always mean them.*

Except…except Cormac seemed to.

He dropped his head forward, lacing his fingers behind his neck. "I don't like to talk feelings."

I smirked. "Few men do."

"Stereotype much?"

I laughed. "Am I wrong?"

He grinned as he shook his head. My heart rate evened out. Teasing I could manage. The heavy emotions… He wasn't the only one twisting in the wind, unable to find his footing.

"Nah. Most dudes I know don't like deep, emotional discussions, especially not with a beautiful woman sitting naked in their bed." He winked. "Can't believe my mother cock blocked me," he muttered. He lifted his head, eyes wide with worry. "I just mean there's no way we'd sex it up tonight."

I raised an eyebrow and dropped my gaze to his now semi-hard dick. "No way?"

He shook his head, expression resolute. "No. Not until you know, without a doubt, that I care about you, that you're the *only* woman I want in my bed."

He strode into his bathroom and shut the door, leaving me to contemplate his coved ceiling and its lack of nasty popcorn bumps.

CHAPTER 33
Keelie

Cormac brought me to the arena early on Saturday to watch the game. The space echoed with the rows of empty seats, and the screens were dark, the ice smooth and unvarnished after the Zamboni tooled through.

"Hey." I turned around when someone tapped my shoulder and looked up a row into the gorgeous smile of a slim, dark-haired woman who could have been a twenty-something Halle Berry.

"Hello," I said.

"You're Keelie, right?"

I nodded, flummoxed.

"Cormac said you'd be here today. I'm Adam's wife, Naomi. Adam's the goalie."

"Oh, yeah, of course. It's great to meet you."

She chuckled as she climbed over the seat next to me and sank into the plush cushion. "That's nice of you to say. I'm a bit much, which you'll discover tonight, I'm sure."

"Um…"

"Cormac wanted to make sure you were happy, having a good time. There are a couple of other girlfriends—the guys call us CATS, which I think is weird and probably misogynistic…" At my confusion, she leaned closer. "Cat's meow. A body part…" Her gaze dropped to her lap.

I gasped. "Oh! Cormac said it stood for comrades, allies, teammates, and spouses."

Naomi cackled. "Sure it does, *officially*. Maybe the team even means it." She tapped her lips. "Okay, I bet the big boss man wanted the name to be more inclusive than just ladies. He's been pretty insistent on ensuring everyone feels like they're part of the organization." She shrugged. "But you know these alpha men love us sitting in the CATS section." She winked.

I didn't know how I felt about Naomi's comments. Actually, yes, I did. I disliked the name—the reason for it. Naomi continued talking, having moved on from the whole hoo-ha explanation.

What was *wrong* with people? Why did everything have to be a ridiculous innuendo?

"The other ladies aren't here tonight," she continued. "Right now, we have ladies and sometimes kids, none of those partners, but I'm a great ally." She winked. "Nicole was super upset to miss out, but she has a cold and stayed home. So, how long have you and Cormac been banging?"

I forced my jaw to stay closed. Gaping was rude. "We're not—"

"Gotcha. Man, your face!" She giggled. "That's twice now you've looked like you're trying to swallow glass. Adam rubbed off on me because I never would have asked that question two years ago. I've always been over the top but not straight-up rude. I'm sorry...didn't mean to embarrass you. And I made up the thing about CATS. Gunnar, the owner, is a great guy, one of the best in the league. He is trying to be more inclusive. Hell, he snapped up the first openly-gay player. I'm waiting for that cutie to find the love of his life and set him up with us here in the CATS section."

"It's fine." Even I heard the stiffness in my tone.

She grabbed my hand. "I am sorry." Her pretty eyes pleaded with me—as if I could say no to her.

"We're good. Really."

"Don't you have a friend? I thought she came with you last time."

I swallowed, my throat heavy. "Marian. She moved." I twisted my fingers in my lap. "It was a shock." I forced down the hurt. "Why don't you tell me a bit about you?"

Naomi smiled, her deep dimples appearing. "Sure! I'm a brand manager for a lingerie boutique. Think Victoria's Secret but more upscale."

"W-wow. That's amazing."

She crinkled her nose and lifted her shoulders. "I know," she squealed. "I love it. All the time, I get to feel feminine and flirty. Even better, Adam loves the products." She winked.

My cheeks warmed again. "Maybe I'll have to stop in sometime."

Her smile was mischievous. "Believe me when I say that Cormac is *more* than happy to pay for whatever confection you want." She waggled her eyebrows.

"No, no, I couldn't ask him to pay—"

"You can and will. That man is hotness personified. All that growly masculinity in a hurt package." She fanned herself. "We've all been waiting to see who he wanted, and you are the sweetest woman possible. I might get a cavity as I repeat your resumé: occupational therapist for a public school, helps at the animal shelter, and runs half marathons for fun."

"I've been running forever." I fiddled with the threads that poked through the small hole in my jeans, high on my thigh. Maybe I should have dressed nicer, like Naomi. She was so put together in her silk capris and mint-green shell. Not that I had the money to spend on high-end brands. I sighed, hating how out of my league I felt. A few patrons had moseyed into the arena, and Naomi bent down to dig in her bag. She pulled out a large jersey with Adam's name and number on it and slipped it over her cute top.

"I came straight from work—we received a rather large order." Her smile grew wider, her eyes gleaming. "And worth getting here later than I'd planned."

"Oh?"

"I hope the client enjoys what I had sent over."

"You send things to people's houses?"

"Everything for a price." She rose. "Want a drink? Some food?"

"Sure." I grabbed my bag and followed her.

Somehow, we returned to our seats with arms laden with food and my wallet untouched. I scowled. "You should have let me pay for something."

"Psssh. I will once you and Cormac are *together* together. For now, let Adam handle our snacks. You give and return." She winked. Plopping back down in her chair, now surrounded by fans, many of whom wore team jerseys or hats, she bit into a doughy pretzel. "Mmm... That's good."

I lowered my voice and leaned in. "I'm not sure how I feel about...well, the wealth."

She swallowed and licked her thumb. When she turned toward

me, her expression was earnest. "It's gross, the amount of money these athletes make. Now, they work *hard*. That's why they play in the NHL. But their salaries are only a part of their income—hell, I'm pretty sure their uniform brand has all these boys on their marketing payroll. They have the money most of us will never dream of. And many of them don't come from wealth themselves, so they either hoard it or they spend, spend, spend. Lucky for me—and you—our guys like to save. And not just for a rainy day."

"But think of all the good that money could do for…for schools or…"

Naomi smiled, but it drooped. "If I've learned one thing in my years, it's that no one is going to give extra money to kids in school. Hell, this crap we're eating now is a million times better than the mayo sandwiches I got for school."

I dropped the last of my snacks into my lap and squeezed her hand. "They wouldn't give you free lunch?"

She shook her head, a hollow laugh barking from her throat. She raised her chin, pride stamped across her features. "My mama wouldn't let me get a free lunch. That was for the grifters and convicts. Nah, I had to make do with whatever we had in the house, which was always nothing…" She trailed off, her posture stiff but her head held high. Still, her lip quivered before she swallowed.

Clearly, I'd struck a nerve. I opened my mouth, planning to apologize, but she waved her hand, as if dissipating the mood. "But that's my point: these boys use their money for good. At least some of it. So, if the school system matters to you, have Cormac get involved in lunches. Nutrition is in an athlete's

wheelhouse. Or PE or after-school activities—there are lots of
ways for him to harness his fame and fundraise bigger bucks."

The arena went dark, and then the announcer began introducing the players.

"Oh, good," Naomi said. "Game time."

She launched into an explanation about the offsides rule, the
one thing I hadn't grasped when Cormac and I talked before.

"That's a hard one," she assured me. "Give it time. You'll get it."

"I'm sorry I upset you. Before," I said.

She shook her head. "You didn't. Not really. I'm just… I get
where you're coming from, and I understand your worry about
the money. It's weird, but it's also so comforting to know I won't
have to live in my family's car, you know?"

I nodded. Never had I considered myself lucky…well, before
now. My childhood had been threadbare and often bleak. My
mother had worked two, sometimes three jobs, which meant she
was never home. But I hadn't ever lived in a car or gone hungry at
school. And now, Naomi was successful in her own right, married
to a sexy athlete.

Cormac skated by, his face intent as he struggled to control the
puck. His powerful body surged as he moved with such speed and
grace. I pressed my hand to my chest, shocked by his effect on me.
I wanted him. And I wanted to attend more games with Naomi.

Cormac slapped a shot into the net, and the arena went
wild—including Naomi and me. I screamed, hugging her.
Cormac fist pumped and pointed toward us. Toward me.

Everything inside me settled as I screamed and waved. In this
moment, it all seemed so clear. I wanted this life with him.

CHAPTER 34
Cormac

Later that night, after the game, Keelie leaned back against the wooden bench in my sauna and moaned. The steam wrapped around her towel-clad nakedness, giving me alluring glimpses of her curves and all that tantalizingly golden skin.

It was late, and we were enjoying some much-needed wind-down time before I took her upstairs. To bed.

Anticipation rippled through me, but I tamped down my need.

"When you told me the other night that you wanted me hot, sweaty, and naked, I was thinking in bed."

I grinned. "I know. But I also told you I wouldn't push you past your comfort zone." I hesitated, blew out a breath. "And we still need to resolve what happened the other night…the picture…"

She glanced down. A bead of sweat rolled from her forehead down her nose. Her features were delicate, but Keelie wasn't fragile.

"You promise that you didn't put the picture there?" she asked.

"I promise."

Her lashes lifted, and the vulnerability in her eyes stole my breath. "And you don't still have feelings for your ex-wife?"

I shook my head. "I don't. Not romantic ones. She's my past." I ran my fingertips along her soft, damp cheek. "You, Keelie, are my future."

She studied me for a long moment. I let her look as deeply

into me as she needed. Opening myself was hard, but she needed the reassurance. I understood that.

"Okay."

"So…we're good?"

She bit her lip, teasing the plump flesh between those small white teeth. "Yeah."

I kissed her, softly, sweetly, letting her know she mattered to me. "Good."

We sat in companionable silence, and I soaked in the moment's peace. I loved being with Keelie because I could just… be. It was freeing and calming. And really fucking nice.

"I've never been in a sauna before," she murmured. Sweat trickled down my bare chest, and she followed the droplets, whimpering when the rivulet hit my towel.

Satisfaction and lust swirled together, much like the heat and stream in the room.

"Now you have."

"This has been quite a weekend—a golf lesson, followed by a golf outing, with my own clubs." She pushed herself up off the bench and sauntered toward me, her bare feet slapping against the smooth pebbles coating the floor. Her towel slid down a little, showing me the entire top swell of those luscious tits. Sweat had blossomed across her skin, making the towel cling to the curve of her waist and the flare of her hip. This woman owned sexy.

She settled on my lap, knees on either side of my hips. I cupped her butt, bringing her forward so her warm center aligned with my now-awakened dick.

"You feel good in my lap," I said.

She wound her arms around my neck. "You look good and feel good."

I slid my hand up along her spine to cup her nape. I leaned forward a little but stopped short of kissing her. She smiled, soft and full of promise as she leaned in the rest of the way, drifting her lips against mine in a sensual glide.

I liked that. A lot.

I used my hand on her back to press her more firmly into my lap as I tipped my head and deepened the kiss.

She hummed and met my advances, nipping and sucking my lower lip when I released her upper one. I groaned, gripping her tighter.

She dropped her hands to my shoulders and dragged her fingertips along my pecs, swirling around my nipples, making them tighten. I ground upward, lightheaded—possibly from the steam but definitely from the effect Keelie had on me.

She scratched downward over my ribs, her fingernails leaving a trail of fire—the carnal kind. I wanted her with a terrible fierceness I struggled to rein in. And with her exploration, with each touch of her tongue to mine, with each shift of her body as she sought to get closer, I knew she wanted me just as badly.

Her damp hair stuck to her temples. I slid my hands along her sides to where the edges of her towel were tucked between her breasts.

"Need to touch you," I mumbled against her lips.

"Please. I want you to."

I tugged the towel apart, and we both moaned long and loud at the contact. I nibbled my way across her cheek, to her jaw, then lower, lower…

Her nipples were pink jewels and her breasts high, plump treasures. I sucked one into my mouth, desperate for more of her.

The timer buzzed.

I wanted to ignore it.

I needed to taste more of Keelie. Her salty-sweet sweat turned me on as much as the hard little nubs topping her gorgeous tits.

But staying in too long could cause us to dehydrate. With a groan, I clasped the sides of her towel, tucking it back between her breasts.

Another chime.

But this one wasn't for the timer.

It was my front door.

The damn universe was reminding me of my promise not to push Keelie too fast, too far. After hurting her once, I had to wait until she trusted me—not just with her body, but with her heart.

CHAPTER 35
Keelie

I gulped in air, but the steam made me even dizzier. Cormac had cost me my common sense. I tried to slide off his lap, but my limbs seemed disjointed—almost as if I were drunk off his taste...or maybe Cormac and the sauna.

"I got you," he murmured. With a soft grunt, he lifted me as he rose from the bench. I rested my cheek against his shoulder, content for the moment to let him hold me. Sweat bloomed wherever we touched—and where we didn't.

He padded out of the room with a confident stride while I clung to him like a baby lemur. No shame from this girl, because he was big and sexy, and I remained woozy. The fresh air revived me a little. So did the incessant chiming of his doorbell.

He pressed a kiss to my temple as he lowered me to the floor. "I'm going to get the door. Want to take a shower?"

I blinked up at him and nodded. He smiled, smoothing back the few strands of hair that clung to my cheek.

"I'm not sure you should try to walk up the stairs. There's a bathroom right here. Towels are in the cabinet. Robes, too. I hope you're okay with the shampoo and stuff, but if not, holler, and I'll see if I can find something else."

"I'll be fine. You need to see who's freaking out at your door."

"I already know it's Maxim," he dipped his head toward a

discreet screen tucked into the bookshelf that ran the length of this wide hall. Cormac's teammate seemed agitated, taking a few jerky steps before turning back to slam his finger against the doorbell yet again.

"Take your time," Cormac said. "When you get out, we can have a snack."

He strode down the hall as I slipped into the bathroom. I turned on the water in the large, glass-walled shower but not to full heat because my body remained warm, thanks to the make-out session on top of the steam. Dropping my towel, I tried not to moan as the fabric slid across my sensitized breasts.

"We might have steamed it up just fine on our own," I muttered as I stepped under the spray. I bit back a squeal as the too-cool water attacked my flesh, splashing over my relaxed muscles.

I turned the hot water up and turned down the cold. Once the water had warmed, I shoved my face into the spray, which helped to clear the haze of lust.

I turned and rinsed my hair, enjoying the large stall. When I squeezed the bottle, the shampoo's scent was woodsier than I preferred, but it smelled clean and crisp, like Cormac, which I liked very much. I finished my hair and smiled as I rubbed the soap over my belly and down my legs. Once clean, I turned off the water and dried off with a big, white fluffy towel before wrapping my tangled hair in it, turban style.

Then I shrugged on the thick robe. I could hear voices—Cormac's deep voice and Maxim's even deeper one coming out in staccato sentences.

I frowned as I opened the door. I picked up my sweaty towel and padded toward their voices.

"I can't leave her alone, not with that monster—Keelie. Hi." Maxim frowned, glancing back and forth between Cormac, who lounged against the counter in just his towel, and me.

His frown deepened. "Sorry. I interrupted. I'll go."

Cormac shot me a look, one full of heat but also apology. "Why don't you ask Keelie what she thinks?"

My eyes widened. "Um, what?"

Cormac slid a glass of something light pink toward me. "Grapefruit juice and seltzer. You need to hydrate after the sauna."

"He didn't tell you the grapefruit is fresh-squeezed," Maxim said. "And that he doesn't share it with anyone. Ever."

Cormac stretched, and I enjoyed the bunching of his muscles, the drink nowhere near as interesting. I took my time, soaking in his thick shoulders and ridged abdominals, down to his hips... My cheeks heated as I noted Cormac's package pressed against the terry cloth. I was aware of his girth, but seeing it, right there, with Maxim in the room... I grabbed the drink and gulped.

"Whoa. You got a cat?" Maxim asked.

Cormac scratched his belly, seemingly unconcerned by his state of undress. "Slippers is Keelie's. Since Keelie's here for the weekend, so is the cat."

He said it like he'd enjoyed moving the litter box and cat food and bowls to his place. Maxim bent down and scratched Slippers under the chin.

He glanced up at us, a smile flirting at the corners of his lips. "She's cute."

Cormac's brows puckered as he noted my heated cheeks. "You okay?"

"Y-yes," I squeaked. "Fine." I took another sip of the drink, desperate for my face to cool. "Just, um, still a little warm." And turned on, which needed to stop. Pronto. "Well, I need to get dressed." I clutched the top of my robe together. Unlike these men, who showered together all season long, I wasn't comfortable without layers of clothing. Whatever Maxim might ask me about would have to wait.

CHAPTER 36
Cormac

I led Keelie down the hall toward my room. Nerves made my belly tumble, but Maxim being here meant Keelie and I wouldn't get carried away. I needed that safeguard.

Once inside my bedroom, I turned toward her. "You know Shannon had an affair with Dukovsky."

She nodded, her brows pinching. "Yes, you told me."

I told her—she hadn't learned from the sports tabloids. Crazy. "Normally, nudity doesn't bother me. I mean, the guys and I change in front of each other every day, but you…being in that robe in front of Maxim… It bothered me. A lot."

She laid her hand on my arm. "I was uncomfortable, too. I'm sure Maxim's nice, but he's not you." She held my gaze, and I saw the honesty there.

I exhaled a harsh sigh. "I didn't realize how much it would bother me. Maybe I should power through—"

"There's nothing wrong with feelings, Cormac." She nibbled her lower lip. "I need to tell you about my parents. And I will, but I will say this now: I don't talk to either of them for very different reasons. Their—our—history is why I've never been in a long-term relationship before, and it's why I get skittish, why I struggle to believe what you tell me."

She needed reassurances from me. I hugged her, rubbing my

hand up and down her back, soothing us both. "I was worried you'd be upset that I was jealous."

"No, I'm relieved. It means you care about me."

"I do."

She smiled. "I'm seeing that. In everything you do."

Leading her into my closet first, I hoped she'd like this surprise. "I got you some things. I hope I did okay. I just wanted to make sure you were comfortable."

She gasped and her fingers pressed to her lips, eyes round as she stared at the couple of shirts, blouses, skirts, and pants I'd neatly arranged on the left side of the closet. They were the only clothes there, making them seem even sparser. I frowned. Maybe I should have bought more...

"You went shopping...for me?"

"Sort of. I called Naomi before the game. I, ah, talked to her about some things for you, and well, I asked her to get a personal shopper from the store next door to pick out a few more things. Just some basics..."

She hugged me so hard, the air puffed past my lips.

"Thank you. Oh, this is so nice! No one's ever done something like this for me."

"You should try something on. I got your sizes when I washed your clothes—"

"It doesn't matter if they fit." She blinked hard as she stepped away, touching the clothes. "It's the thought. Y-you've done so much for me..."

She turned again and threw herself into my arms. I held her close as she sniffled.

"Are you okay?" I whispered.

"I'm happy."

"Oh."

"And I don't like to cry, but you've overwhelmed me this weekend. First, the golf, now this—"

I shifted so I could see her expression. Her towel slid from her hair, leaving the long strands framing her face. Eyes sparkling with tears, the tip of her nose red, hair needing a brushing…she was beautiful. Stunning. I wanted this woman in my closet, but more importantly, in my life, every day.

"I want you happy, pretty girl. You deserve all the happiness."

This time, her smile started in her eyes. They sparkled brighter than any gem, and they captivated me. I caught my breath. In that moment, I fell all the way in love with Keelie Hayes.

While Keelie dressed, I sped through my shower. She knocked on the bathroom door to tell me she was heading back downstairs. She was so thoughtful about my issues. I needed to be the same about hers. She was opening up to me. I just needed patience until she told me everything.

I hated the mere *idea* of patience.

I tugged on my underwear and sweatpants before grabbing a shirt, which I shrugged over my too-damp chest as I hurried back to the kitchen…and found Maxim and Keelie leaning on my kitchen island. She rolled her glass of grapefruit spritzer between her hands, mouth gaping as she hung on Maxim's every word.

"Whoa… He tried to hit her?"

Maxim growled. "He did."

Keelie gasped. "That's so scary!"

"That's why I want her to stay with me."

"Wait. I'm missing something. Do you know her? Like, before last weekend?"

Maxim shook his head.

"But you want her to move in with you?"

I came to stand next to Keelie, and she immediately shifted her weight to press herself into my side. I wrapped an arm around her waist, enjoying the warmth of her body. She'd chosen a pair of shorts and a flowy top with sleeves that ended just past her elbows, and she'd pulled her damp hair into a messy bun. I kissed her temple, and she turned to smile at me.

I could get lost in those big, blue eyes.

Maxim sighed. "He threatened her. Knows where she lives. The cops can't do anything until he hurts her. I have good security. Better than her place. I can make sure that…twerp…doesn't bother her."

Keelie took another sip of her drink before she asked, "What does she want to do?"

"Ida Jane says she doesn't want to impose. How can one small woman in a guest room cause more imposition than my head refusing to stay in the game? Huh? You talk to her. Make her see reason. Please, Keelie. I don't want her to be hurt."

Maxim Dolov, one of the biggest D-men in the league, blinked at Keelie with these fucking puppy-dog eyes, and she melted. "I guess I could talk to her."

Maxim rose to his full height. "Yes! Yes, make her see I'm going to help her."

"B-but why?"

He tugged on his upper lip. Finally, he shrugged. "It's the right thing to do."

"Call her," I said.

Maxim fiddled with his phone, then set it on the counter between us.

"Hello?" a sugary voice asked. It was low and warm, like honey drizzled over a Fredericksburg peach. Maxim seemed to think so, too, because his expression turned just as syrupy.

Wow. Max was into this woman.

"Hi, Ida Jane. I know you don't know me," Keelie said. She seemed nervous. Maxim shifted, made a go-on gesture. "My name's Keelie Hayes. I know Maxim through Cormac Bouchard. He's—"

"Her man," I said, liking the title I'd given myself. The edginess surrounding Maxim remained, and he almost vibrated as he stared at the phone.

"How many of you are there?" Ida Jane asked.

"There's me, Cormac, and Maxim," Keelie said. "Maxim came by because he's so worried about your safety—"

"These men. I gotta tell you, Keelie. They are gettin' on my last nerve. I mean, threatening my life—"

"Whoa. Wait. Who threatened you?" Keelie asked. Her face scrunched, and her fists balled. My woman was all protective fire.

"My shitty ex. But that's not the point. I can't move in with a man I don't know."

"I get your concern," Keelie said. She glanced up at me, a soft smile gracing those soft, kiss-swollen lips. "But I have to say that when these hockey players decide on something, there's no changing their mind."

"Well, Maxim coulda asked me to keep on stayin' instead of demanding it."

Keelie raised an eyebrow and shot Maxim a look. "Yes, he could have." This time, Keelie used that teacher voice I found so damn hot.

Maxim, sensing his scheming was about to head south, scooped up his phone, punched a button, and walked out of the kitchen toward the pool deck. His tone seemed designed to placate.

CHAPTER 37
Keelie

Cormac shook his head, brow scrunched. "I've never seen him like this about a woman."

"Sounds like she went through something pretty traumatic."

"Maxim's a protector. I know he gets a bad rap as the out-of-control fighter, but that's because he hates to see others hurt, especially those unwilling to fight back."

I touched the tassel at the end of the tunic I wore. It was flowy but also semi-sheer, which is why I'd paired it with a camisole. Cormac had purchased me a few lingerie sets that were frillier and of much higher quality than I would have bought myself. Slipping them on made me feel feminine, sexy.

Softness swirled through me as I looked him over. Such a large man, both in height and muscle, he was also kind. No, *gentle*. A true gentle man. A good one. I worried the tassel, wondering when he'd realize he was far above my pay grade—not just financially but as a would-be partner.

"So, he's reacting to her because she was hurt?" I frowned. That wasn't a good reason to be with someone.

Cormac pulled out a *charcuterie* board from the fridge. "No, I don't think so."

"So, he's attracted to her, but then her ex threatened her, and he wants to help."

He popped a slice of salami into his mouth.

"That seems more likely."

"Well, I want to meet her," I said.

He bit into a slice of cheese, his jaw working as he chewed. I resisted the urge to kiss him.

"Of course. I'll talk to Maxim."

"You don't think he'll mind?" I asked.

He settled the plates on the counter and placed his hands on my shoulders. "Even if he does, I'll make sure you get to meet Ida Jane."

My ears rang. No way this could be my life. It was… It was so perfect. I dropped the tassel and took Cormac's hand. "Why?"

"Because you matter to me, and I want you to be happy."

We spent the rest of that night cuddled together in bed. While I'd hoped Cormac would pick up where we'd left off in the sauna, he seemed content to hold me. I, however, wanted more. I just didn't know how to tell him. He had already been married, and I didn't know how to do anything related to a relationship.

I lay awake for a long time, trying to wrap my head around the unevenness of our romantic lives. Cormac didn't understand how deep my issues ran because I hadn't told him. I had to explain my past. Soon. I should have done it already. But I didn't want him to look at me the way my father had—like I was nothing. Unwanted. Unlovable.

In the morning, Cormac rose long before I did. He'd worked out and made breakfast before I finally got up. After we ate, we took a Sunday morning swim in his pool. His expression burned with lust when I came out in the swimsuit he'd bought me—a tiny bikini where the blue triangles barely covered my breasts and sex.

"You are stunning," he said, his voice hoarse with emotion.

I slid into the warm water next to him as the sun pounded on our heads. The air had turned muggy; I expected an afternoon rain shower. But for now, the sky was a watery blue.

"Want to show me how much you like it?" I asked. My heart pounded. I struggled with being so forward, but I wanted his arms around me. I craved his body over mine, making me his.

He bit into his soft, kissable lower lip and groaned. "I don't know how I'm going to keep my hands off you."

I frowned. "Why would you want to?"

He tugged off his sunglasses, clearly aware we needed no barriers between us.

"Because I made you a promise, pretty girl. And you need to know I'll always keep my promises to you."

My chest warmed. When he lifted his hand and ran his fingers down my cheek, that heat seemed to radiate outward, heating parts of me that had always been jagged and cold. He kissed my temple, and tears clouded my vision. "Cormac, I…"

He kissed me, and I clung to him, kissing him back even as tears dripped from my lashes.

After some very satisfying pool time, he plucked me from the water and wrapped me in a towel. He held me, nuzzling my hair.

Those jagged bits cracked, and I clung to him, my mind spinning, my heart aching. But each time I opened my mouth to share the reason I struggled with trust, I remembered my father's voice, the look of disgust when he'd told me I was a mistake.

I curled tighter into Cormac, unable to bear the thought of him looking at me like that.

We showered, and I put on more of the clothes Cormac had bought for me. Then he played with Slippers while I made lunch. He'd offered, but I wanted to get to know his kitchen. I liked the layout. It was intuitive and luxurious.

After we ate and Cormac cleaned up, I rubbed my hands on my hips. "I need to go home," I told him. Melancholy weighed on me because I didn't want to leave. "I have reports I have to finish."

Cormac nodded. We packed up Slippers and her stuff, and he drove me back to my house. Sadness filled me. I tipped my head back on the headrest, my eyes scratchy and my throat clogged with tears I couldn't shed. This wasn't goodbye, I reminded myself. "So, what's next week hold?" I asked.

"Let me think…" Cormac frowned, mentally going through his schedule. "We play Montreal next. There. That's on Tuesday."

"Okay."

"I need to talk to my mom about her message to you, and about us in general, so I asked Coach if I could travel ahead of the team. I leave tomorrow morning, early."

"Okay."

"You'll call me?" he asked.

"If you want."

He reached over and grabbed my hand, placing it high on his thigh. "I do. I always want to talk to you. I may not answer, but I'll call you when I can."

"Then I'll call."

Silence returned. *I should tell him about my childhood, make him understand my fears...* He turned onto my street, and I stared at my small house, so different from Cormac's estate. I looked down at my hands twisted in my lap. Now wasn't the time. He had to leave early.

"And you'll be back when?" I asked.

He sighed. "We have another away game on Wednesday, so not until Thursday. Probably mid-day."

I sucked in a breath. "I'm going to miss you."

He leaned in, his hand cupping my jaw, his forehead touching mine. "Not as much as I'll miss you, pretty girl."

"I wish..." I licked my lips and forced myself to be brave, though my stomach twisted. Baby steps. *Tell him this so you can tell him more.* "When you get back, do you think you'll want me to stay with you again?"

His smile widened and his eyes sparkled, tossing off the same melancholy that tortured me. "I'd love that. In fact, I'm going to dream about you in my bed."

Our lips brushed. "It's a date."

"One I'm going to be looking forward to. Very much."

"Me, too."

"I'll help you with Slippers."

Once we'd settled the cat and her stuff inside, Cormac kissed me, slow and sweet, while the cicadas hummed in the background. When he returned to his car, I slid back inside my house, already missing him. My quiet house was tidy...and altogether lonely. I moped around, trying to concentrate on work until I could finally get ready for bed.

CHAPTER 38
Keelie

Cormac texted the next morning to let me know he'd arrived in Montreal. After a brief exchange, he signed off, letting me know he expected the conversation with his mother to be "strained." I hated the idea of creating a wedge between Cormac and his family, and I worried over it most of the day.

Though I missed Cormac, Andy's cuteness perked me up when I got to school. "I can tie my own shoes!" he exclaimed, pride dripping off each word. Then he showed me.

I crouched down next to him. "Wow. You're so good at that! I'm proud of you." I smiled. Andy hugged me, and I squeezed him back. If I'd had someone like me in my life when I was little and struggling, would my father have stayed? I would never know.

I took Andy's hand and led him to the table and chairs. "Do you think you can grasp the pencil like I showed you before? Like this?" I'd shown him a different hold that I thought might improve his control and penmanship.

We continued to work on his writing, and once my session with him ended, the foggy sadness resettled.

At lunch, I checked my phone to find a video from Cormac that showed Naese plowing headfirst into the net, cursing a blue streak.

I laughed as I responded. Once I set down my phone, it rang, and I answered, assuming it was Cormac.

"Hello?"

"Heya, Kee! It's Naomi. How ya doing?"

Disappointment settled in my chest. I missed Cormac too much. He'd given me a fairy-tale weekend, and I struggled to regain my normal equilibrium.

"Okay. You?"

"Great! I got in an hour of Peloton this morning. So, hey, I wanted to invite you to my watch party tomorrow night. Nicole and Doris are coming along with my sister. She's got the hots for...well, all the single boys, but definitely Maxim."

"Maxim is with Ida Jane," I said. I stared down at my carrot sticks. *Not my place to say anything about other people's lives.*

"The girl he met? Oh, if you have her digits, invite her, too. I'll shoot you the address. Bring something for a spa night, 'kay? We meet an hour early to get our masks on and deep conditioner in. I hate to miss any of the game."

"Um..."

"Please come. The girls want to meet you, and I've been dying to find out what you thought about the clothes Cormac got you."

The bell rang, saving me from further embarrassment.

"I have to go, Naomi. But yes. Yes, I'll be there!"

I called Ida Jane that afternoon, after school ended, once I got her number from Maxim. He'd grumbled his concern about her reaction.

"Hi, Ida Jane, this is Keelie," I began.

"Keelie! How are you?"

"Good. So, I was wondering… Would you like to meet up?"

"Yeah, I would." She blew out a noisy breath.

"Great. Where are you?"

She explained, and it was not too far from me—a minor miracle. Houston was a massive city, covering hundreds of miles.

"You wanna grab a bite?" Ida Jane asked.

"Sure. What do you prefer?"

"Oh, hon, I just like to eat."

I considered. Cormac didn't like Tex-Mex, so I needed to get my fix when he was out of town. "Ninfa's?"

Ida Jane hummed. "My favorite."

I smiled. "See you there."

I strolled into the restaurant with a belly full of nerves. What if Ida Jane judged me like Marian had? What if…

"Keelie!"

A small blonde waved from the other side of the crowd, her smile wide and infectious. An enormous bruise swelled around her eye and left cheek. I rushed over, landing on the balls of my feet.

"Hi," I said, breathless.

Ida Jane had a thick sprinkle of freckles on her nose and her non-swollen eye—the only one I could see—was blue. She reminded me of that quintessential cheerleader from all the '90s TV shows. Her accent thickened the more nervous she became, an endearing quality. She was also tiny—maybe five feet tall, and she was the one person I knew who seemed she would fit into an extra small.

"Oh, man, those social media posts didn't do you justice," Ida

Jane said. She laughed, a tinkling sound of happiness. "You're much more of a knockout in person."

I tipped my chin toward her bruised cheek and black eye. "Looks like someone tried to knock you out."

She scowled. "My ex." She ran her fingers around the edge. "I shoulda stayed with Maxim." She pursed her lips. "Instead, it's a hotel for me tonight."

"No way! You can stay with me."

Before she could answer, a server led us to our table. She settled into the booth and leaned her arms on the top, leaning forward.

"I don't think that's a good idea," she said. She spoke louder than normal, thanks to the increase in chatter. Houstonians liked to eat out, and they loved their Tex-Mex.

My excitement about us getting along fizzled. She must have seen the hurt radiating from me.

"Not because I don't like you," she clarified. "I do. But you don't have security." Her breath stuttered from her lips. "And I need it." Dark, ugly memories filled her eyes.

The waiter came over. Much as I wanted a margarita, I still had work to complete tonight, so I settled for a Corona and lime. Ida Jane ordered the same, along with the beef fajitas.

"I come from West Texas. A ranch," she said.

Remembering Cormac's healthy, nutrient-packed meals, I ordered the mole salmon.

"Tell me about this guy," I said. I gestured toward her cheek. "The ex. And Maxim."

As we worked our way through the chips and dip, then our main course, Ida Jane caught me up.

When our plates were clean, I wiped my lips and tossed my napkin on the table. "You're not going to a hotel," I said.

"I don't have anywhere else to go—"

"You do," I said. I sucked in a deep breath. "You can stay with me or—" I raised my hand when she opened her mouth. "I can call Cormac and ask him to let us stay at his place. It has good security."

She glanced down at her lap. "I don't know. I'm not used to taking…"

"I get that. These guys are a whole new level, both of intensity and lifestyle. But they also care."

She licked her lips. "I'm scared. And I feel alone."

My heart thrummed. Those were words I should have said to Cormac. Ida Jane, a woman who barely knew me, had already opened up more to me than I had to the man who'd shown me romance…and love.

Yes, love.

And I'd already fallen hard for him.

CHAPTER 39
Cormac

I sat in my mother's kitchen, staring at the rooster wallpaper that had graced the walls since the late '90s. It peeled a little in places, but overall, the house was immaculate—a time capsule of my teenage years. My trophies continued to sit in the glass-front case in the living room. Pictures from my wedding to Shannon were on the mantel.

Nothing had changed since my last visit—least of all my mother's ridiculous belief that Shannon and I would reconcile and start popping out grandbabies.

She'd even brought out a list of names—names!—for these kids I'd never have.

I didn't want a family with Shannon, not now. And I didn't want my parents involved in my potential kids' lives—not if they were this unbending about my happiness.

And I was sure I never wanted my mother to talk to Keelie. I remained unsure of how badly her parents' failed marriage had wounded Keelie, but clearly their selfishness had hurt her. I refused to allow my mother's narrow views to do more damage.

I loved Keelie too much to put her feelings at risk. And my mother would not change her mind about Keelie. I was becoming more certain of that by the moment.

I turned to face my mother again. "You're saying it doesn't

matter that I love Keelie. That I want a future with her?"

"She's not your wife. Shannon is," my mother said. She sat stiff and straight in her chair. My dad hunched in his. Why did he put up with her BS?

Why had I? "She asked me for a divorce, which I granted, and Shannon doesn't want kids," I told her again. "Hell, she doesn't want me. We're not right for each other. I see that now."

"She always loved you, Mac," my mother said, as if I hadn't spoken. "And as for the children… You were young."

"And you wouldn't stop pushing," I snapped.

"Don't speak to your mother like that," Dad said.

Of the two of them, Dad was more level-headed. These days he was a grayer, paunchier version of me, and I didn't love the peek into my future. My father wasn't a wicked man, but he'd devoted his life to my successes, which meant he'd given up his own chance at living.

As much as I cared about them, they would not hear me. What a waste of time.

I rose. "I won't again."

I hesitated before leaning down to kiss my mother's weathered cheek. "Goodbye."

"Bye? What do you mean?" Mom asked.

Taking a deep breath, I said, "I won't be coming back because I won't bring Keelie here to be treated like something lesser because of your prejudices. So, I'm telling you goodbye."

"Cormac…" My father's tone held a warning.

I shook my head. "You've made your choices, and they're never about what's best for *me*."

Once I left their house, a weight seemed to lift. I might love my parents, but I didn't want to experience their myopia any longer. Maybe in time we'd rebuild a relationship that worked for all of us. Maybe we wouldn't. Either way, I'd tried.

I drove my rental car back to the hotel and found my room—a posh space with soft lighting and two King beds covered in silky duvets in a sleek, dark gray. I went to the gym almost immediately, as I needed an hour to work out the frustration I felt after visiting my parents. I had a little more breathing room now. The rest of the guys would show up in the next half hour or so, and then we'd grab dinner. Good thing because I was starving.

My phone rang just before I hopped into the shower. I smiled as I brought it to my ear, my earlier frustrations fading. "Keelie."

"Hi, Cormac."

I loved her voice. I loved that she'd called me. I loved her. As soon as I came up with a romantic plan, I'd tell her so, too. I wanted to make sure she never forgot the first time I told her how I felt…I didn't want to forget either.

I frowned, noting the background noise. "You sound like you're out."

"Ida Jane and I met up at Ninfa's."

"Oh. Are you having fun?"

"Yes. I like her."

"Good."

Keelie sucked in a long breath. "I need a favor."

I settled back against the room's armchair, wincing a little as my hamstring pulled. "Of course," I said. This was the first time

Keelie had asked for something, and I would do everything in my power to make it happen.

"Can I...we...Ida Jane and me...stay at your place?"

That was her favor? "I'd love you to be there." I smiled, liking the idea of Keelie in my house, sleeping in my bed. "But why the change of heart?"

Keelie lowered her voice. "Her ex hit her."

I sucked in a breath. "Does Maxim know?"

"I didn't ask. But she won't stay with me. She said she needs security—"

"Then hell yes, you're staying at my place. I can even bring in a bodyguard—"

"Whoa! That's unnecessary. For me. I don't know how Ida Jane feels. I want her safe."

I blew out a breath. "Maxim and I will coordinate security," I said, voice tight. I rose from the bed and paced. Much as I loved Maxim, his girl had better not put mine in danger.

"I don't want you worried about me," Keelie said, as if reading my mind. "You need to focus on winning your games."

"I can do that better if I know you're safe."

She was quiet for a moment. "I worry you're too good to be true."

That tone again. Whatever dark secret Keelie held, it had to do with someone important not loving her, protecting her, and that first someone *had* to have been her father. My lip curled.

People could be so selfish, so damn hurtful. My parents' view of the world had stopped them from having a relationship with me... Being back in that house had been stifling. Our conversa-

tion—or lack thereof—had created more tension because I knew
they hadn't heard me today. But I'd made my choice clear, and if
needed, I'd deal with them later. Right now, Keelie needed me.

I chuckled as I thought about her comment. "You wouldn't
worry about that if you knew what I was thinking."

She exhaled, clearly relieved. "I'll have to bring Slippers back."

"Good. I like her. You know that. I'll text you the code to the
gate, and I'll have my assistant swing by my place now with a key."

"Cormac…"

So many emotions welled up in me when she said my name
like that. Keelie finally seemed to understand how much I wanted
to take care of her.

"Thank you."

"You're welcome. One of these days, you're going to realize
what I keep telling you: you're important to me."

I could hear the smile in her voice. "I'm beginning to."

CHAPTER 40
Keelie

"I'm not sure how you talked me into this," Ida Jane said when I picked her up from work the next evening. We drove to Naomi's, where we planned to watch the game. She tugged at her top, then at her hair, embarrassed by the bruises on her cheek and jaw and the impressive shiner that still appeared swollen and tender around her eye.

"Well, I'm new, too, so I figured we'd be freaked out together," I told her. "Plus, you're my roomie now." I smiled as I turned at Naomi's—also Cormac's—street. I'd learned many of the guys lived in the same neighborhood. That made getting home afterward easy.

I still wasn't sure exactly what was going on with Ida Jane and Maxim, but she'd allowed the bodyguard who showed up this morning to drive her to work. He would have brought her back to Cormac's, too, but I'd needed to run errands after school and that put me near her office. Instead, Ida Jane's bodyguard now followed behind us in his SUV. Maybe I should have let him drive us here, but I didn't understand how all this security stuff worked.

"You're dating Cormac. Well, I guess right now, you're living with him, right?"

A thrill went through me, and I smiled. I'd missed Cormac's house, missed him. And I'd slept well, snuggled into sheets that

smelled of him—much better than the night before when I'd
tossed and turned, missing him. I also slept in one of his shirts,
wanting him as close as possible.

"I'm just Maxim's feel-good project," Ida Jane muttered. She
slumped down in the seat.

"That isn't true. Maxim told us he likes you." I chewed on my
lip. "I'm nervous. Naomi's fun, but she's loud and asks a lot of
questions…"

Ida Jane perked up. "I have an enormous family with tons of
nosy women. Those I know how to handle. Consider me your
wing woman."

I sighed and nodded. "That would be amazing. I think Naomi
and I could be great friends…once I figure out how to handle her."

Ida Jane made a sound. "Don't make me laugh. The bruises
hurt."

I winced. "Sorry."

Naomi and Adam's house was a larger and more ostentatious
version of Cormac's. I parked a few feet behind a sleek foreign car
that looked new. My chest tightened, and I glanced over at Ida
Jane, glad to see that she, too, seemed off-kilter.

"This isn't my world," she mumbled.

"I totally understand," I said. "I'm a public school employee."

Before we'd even exited the car, Naomi pulled the wood-
and-mullion glass door open and waved with her right hand,
a margarita in her left. She wore a romper that flowed over her
figure with glitzy sandals.

"This is going to be crazy," I said, glancing back to the
driveway. Ida Jane's bodyguard nodded at me. I waved.

"I think you're right."

I grabbed the tote with spa stuff I'd picked up after work yesterday and got out. I slammed the door shut, wincing as it squeaked.

"Yay, you're here! Nicole brought a margarita machine, so that's going to mean loose lips and a hangover tomorrow." Naomi's grin faded as she caught sight of Ida Jane's battered face.

"Who the hell did this to you?" she demanded.

"My ex—"

"Did Maxim beat the shit out of him?" She remained stiff, her expression furious. She looked, in that moment, as if the lightest touch would cause her to shatter. Naomi usually seemed devil-may-care, but her absolute focus on Ida Jane's injuries felt personal.

Ida Jane shook her head. Her pale skin whitened, causing the swirls of purples, blues, and yellows to stand out even more starkly.

"No, the rat bastard ran away cuz he's a cowardly sack of horseshit. No offense to horses."

Naomi sniffed, her disdain clear in every line of her expression and body. "Horses should be offended. When the police find him, I want a turn." She curled her lip, anger vibrating off her. "My boyfriend in college hit me. If Mimi hadn't come home in time…" She guzzled her margarita.

"I'm sorry that happened to you," Ida Jane said, touching Naomi's shoulder.

The two shared a long look, and then Naomi nodded. Whatever passed between them cementing a bond. I shifted, unsure what to say.

After a moment, Naomi brightened. "Sorry, that was a lot for the welcome committee. Come on in. Hey, girls! Keelie's here with Maxim's CAT." Naomi winked. "Mimi, be sure to lay off on the questions. Ida Jane's face got stomped."

Mimi turned out to be a younger, more curvaceous version of Naomi. She hugged both Ida Jane and me and chattered pretty much nonstop about nothing. But she was sweet and thoughtful, happy to ask and answer her own questions. She reminded me of a hummingbird, flitting around the room in her pretty clothes, her big eyes sparkling.

"I'm Nicole," a sleek brunette said. "I'm Quentin's wife. He's one of the D-men." She walked in from the open-concept living area toward the kitchen, where the rest of us stood. The spaces were large and ornate. The wood floors were polished and covered in thick rugs while the farmhouse-style kitchen boasted soft blue walls and dark wood farm doors. A huge TV took up most of one wall in the living area, a gas fireplace another, and windows the last one. Three large white leather couches were situated to ensure an optimal TV-watching experience.

Once Nicole shook both our hands, she pulled her hair up into a messy bun and dug through the bag I'd brought. "Ooh, Keelie's my new favorite person," she said. "She went to Sephora."

I shuffled, wondering if I'd made a mistake. Wanting to impress these women now seemed foolish. They were nice and made me feel welcome. Still, they were married to professional athletes, living in enormous homes, and driving brand-new cars. My salary only stretched so far—and I'd stretched it this month to bring this bag of goodies.

"Lemme see." Naomi hip-checked Mimi, her sister, and dove into the bag headfirst.

Ida Jane inched closer to me, probably because I was familiar. "Do they do this for every away game?"

I shrugged.

"No," Nicole said. "But we like to when we can. Quentin and I have three kids, and I like to be there at bedtime because he can't. But he's about to retire—or be forced to, thanks to his shoulder." She grimaced. "And he's not happy about it. He's going to want to stay in the industry, and we both like the club here. We're hoping Coach Whittaker and Gunnar Evaldson—that's the Wildcatters' owner—will ask him to stay on as a defensive coach, but we haven't gotten there yet."

"The thing you have to know about hockey is that the roster changes pretty much every year," Naomi said. She opened one of the exfoliating creams I'd brought and sniffed. "You didn't need to go this all-out, but we're going to appreciate how great our skin looks."

"Did you see this eye cream?" Nicole asked, signaling that she didn't want to talk more about her husband's transition and the potential move that would upend her family. "Girls, our men are going to lose their minds when they see us on Thursday."

"Let's get you girls some drinks and dive into these cosmetics," Naomi said.

"So, how's life with Cormac?" Naomi asked during a commercial.

We'd eaten delicious vegetarian tacos, and I'd now switched to sparkling water since I had to drive back to Cormac's—the entire quarter or half a mile. Still, I refused to get behind the wheel if I was even the tiniest bit tipsy.

"Good. I'm staying there. With Ida Jane."

"That was fast." Naomi chuckled. "Good for you, Keelie! I didn't think you had it in you."

I picked at a thread on my knee. These jeans were about to rip open—and not in the I-paid-a-lot-of-money-for-artful-tearing way. No, mine split from normal wear. Marian's comment that I had no sense of style flooded my mind. I swallowed, insecurities clogging my throat.

"I…I'm falling in love with him, but I don't know what to do."

Suddenly, everyone focused on me. The game resumed on the enormous screen, but the women seemed to edge closer.

"What's going on?" Nicole asked.

My heart fluttered. "I found a picture of him with his ex in his bedside drawer right when…" I dropped my head into my hands, face burning, and mumbled the rest.

"Damn," Mimi said.

"And that would have been your first time together?" Naomi asked.

"Yeah. I mean, kind of?" I licked my lips, refusing to say more. "We talked about it later, but now, I'm afraid…"

Naomi took a big sip of her drink. "Girl, you need the horizontal mambo."

"Might ruin her for other men," Nicole mused.

Naomi scoffed. "Of course it will. He's a professional athlete. They have to fuck like they play—all out."

Ida Jane took my hand, and I appreciated her silent support.

"Why, Keelie?" she asked. "I know you have a good reason." When the women turned their attention to Ida Jane, she flushed but lifted her chin. "I'm not ready to jump into bed or a relationship with Maxim, so I appreciate that y'all are taking things slower."

I squeezed her hand, thankful for her presence here. I liked Ida Jane a lot. She had a deep strength, steel will under the softness of a Southern accent. Ida Jane was the real deal, genuine to her convictions. And I liked that she had Maxim in a tangle. These men were used to getting what they wanted when they wanted it. Cormac hadn't seemed to let that go to his head, but it had to shape his—their—expectations. Like Ida Jane and Naomi, I wanted to continue to be me, with my career and interests, even if I also wanted a relationship with Cormac. And I wanted that with a deep, terrible hunger.

Naomi flopped back and turned toward the screen. The Wildcatters had the puck. Cormac passed it forward to Naese as someone on the other team brought his stick up and sent Cormac sprawling.

A moment later, Maxim slammed the player into the boards.

"Sounds to me like you need to talk to each other," Naomi said, turning back to face me, her expression serious. "Adam and I usually have deep conversations on the phone—something about not having to look at each other helps, I think." She shrugged. "But I tell him all the stuff that frightens me, leaves me feeling weak, vulnerable. It's harder for him, but he's trying. And he's protective of the scared me that just needs some good loving."

"Oh, you turned it into a joke," Mimi complained. "And you'd been doing so well."

Nicole took a sip of her drink, contemplating me over the rim. "Don't we all have baggage? I was a single mother before Quentin and I began dating. Naomi had an abusive ex. Cormac's ex flaunted her one-night stand with the league's resident asshole."

"I don't like her," I muttered.

"Neither do we," Naomi said. "She's big for her britches." She shot Ida Jane a wink, and she giggled.

"My point is Naomi's right: you have to talk those uncomfortable, scary bits through," Nicole said. "Especially the hard feelings. These men travel about half the time, and women throw themselves at them constantly." She frowned, as did Naomi and Mimi.

Naomi shook her head. "I hate when women do that to each other. And I hate that Adam slept with so many of them." She grimaced. "But I can't change his past, so I accept it. Sometimes it sticks in my throat and makes me gag. But I try. Because I love him." Her lovely eyes turned softer, dreamier. "And he loves me. Takes such good care of me."

"When you're ready, have the sexy times." Nicole winked. "Cormac will rock your world—"

"And then you can tell us about it, and I can live vicariously through you," Mimi piped in.

I wrinkled my nose. "I'm not telling you details of my sex life."

"You'd have to be having sex to have a sex life," Naomi pointed out.

"Well, aren't you Ms. Semantics?" I shook my head. "Do you want to watch the game or not?" I motioned to the television. "Looks like the Wildcatters just scored."

Naomi scrambled for the remote.

CHAPTER 41
Cormac

After our two-one win against Montreal, I tromped out after the guys, looking forward to a celebratory drink. Settled in at the bar, I sipped my beer, enjoying the accolades and backslaps from my teammates.

Pete sent me a text: *Great goal. Bet it felt good to get one on Dukovsky.*

It did. Not going to lie, but I thought about Keelie. I knew, from both her and Adam, that she'd watched the game with Naomi, Mimi, Nicole, and Ida Jane.

"If they scared off Ida Jane, I'm going to beat you to a pulp," Maxim growled, shooting daggers at Adam and Quentin. He set his empty beer glass on the counter and stormed off, phone to his ear.

"I guess he really likes her," Adam said, eyes wide.

I nodded. "Guess so." A hand brushed my arm, squeezing my biceps. I turned, already tugging myself away. "Oh, Shannon," I said as I realized who it was. I hugged her, just like I always had. "Nice to see you."

"I wanted to congratulate you on beating your former team." Her smile turned strained. "And also on your new relationship."

I leaned against the bar, nonplussed that she'd wrangled her way into our group. "Thank you. I'm happy with both those scenarios."

She winced. "We didn't leave things all that well when I was in Houston—"

"I thought we did."

She searched my gaze, her eyes wide and filled with…was that yearning? No, I must be mistaken.

"Your mother called me."

I grimaced. "Let me guess, to tell you we're still married in the eyes of the church. I heard the same crap."

Shannon licked her lower lip. Her lipstick was a shade darker than their natural color. She'd always liked, as she put it, a "full face." Shannon looked good, but Keelie's smooth skin dotted with the occasional freckle popped into my mind. Keelie didn't cover herself like she was going to war, like Shannon did.

"What if it isn't crap?" she asked.

My phone rang, and I yanked it from my pocket. Whatever Shannon and my mother had cooked up, I wasn't interested in pursuing, as I'd told my mom yesterday. "This is Keelie. Good to see you, Shannon." I put the phone to my ear and pushed through the crowd, much as Maxim had a few minutes ago. "Hello?"

"Cormac? Is now a bad time?"

"No, of course not. Are you at my place?"

"Yeah."

I smiled. "Good. I like that you're there. Hang on—Maxim's about to get in a Lyft." I pulled the phone from my ear. "Are you heading back to the hotel?" I asked.

Maxim nodded. "Yeah. It's too loud in there to talk to Ida Jane."

"Good. Let's go," I said.

Maxim's scowl grew. "Aw, man, I can't talk to her if you're in the car."

"So's the driver," I pointed out.

He scowled. "Fine. But…don't fuck this up for me."

"How could I?"

I slipped into the back seat and returned the phone to my ear. "Okay, I'm back. Maxim and I are headed to the hotel."

"Oh? Where were you?" Keelie asked.

"We went to a bar to celebrate our win." I frowned. "Shannon came in and wanted to talk, so I'm even more glad you called."

Keelie was quiet for a long moment. "What did she want to talk about?"

"I'm not sure. I wasn't interested."

The silence dragged on again. "I…don't know how I feel about her seeking you out."

"I do. I'm annoyed."

Another pause. We pulled up in front of the hotel, and I exited the car with a wave to the driver.

"I'm jealous," Keelie whispered. "And I don't like how that feels."

"You have no reason to be jealous."

A couple of young men ran toward us, asking for photos and autographs. Much as I wanted to ignore them, that wasn't Wild-catters policy. "Can I call you back when I make it to my room? It'll be just a minute."

"That's okay—"

"I'll call you as soon as I'm upstairs," I said, my tone firm. Keelie was already worried about my relationship with Shannon.

That's why I'd flown up here before the rest of the team—to cut my mother's meddling off at the roots. My mind whirred over how best to handle Shannon's newfound interest in my life.

I finished the photo session and signed another autograph, noting Maxim's heavy scowl as we walked into the hotel. We bee-lined to the elevators.

"What's up with you?" I asked.

"Ida Jane's being difficult."

"About?"

He shook his head. We rode up to the tenth floor in silence, both of us more interested in the conversations with our women than with each other.

"See you tomorrow," I said as I slid my keycard into the door. As soon as it was closed, I pulled out my phone and dialed Keelie back. "Okay, I'm in my room. Now, I wanted to tell you that you have nothing to be jealous about. Especially with Shannon. You're the one in my house, sleeping in my bed."

Her breath hitched.

I plowed on. "Right where I want you. Except I wish I was there with you. I miss you, pretty girl."

"Okay."

"You sure?"

"Well, I mean…I'm seeing a new photo of you two hugging, but if you say there's nothing between you, I…I believe that. You've never lied to me."

She trusted me. Thank *fuck*. I'd needed to know that. There was no way we could take our relationship further without a firm foundation of trust.

"And I never will."

Another long pause.

"Why do I feel like something's weighing on you?" I asked. I toed off my shoes and dropped onto my bed, staring up at the ceiling.

"Because there is. Naomi and Nicole said I should talk to you. About…about my past. It's not a pretty story. But I need to give you the real reason I struggle so much to believe you're not too good to be true."

CHAPTER 42
Keelie

Cormac's voice came over the phone line. "I want to know about you, Keelie. All about you. Even the not-pretty parts."

I choked on a laugh that was almost a sob. With a firm press of my lips, I held down further eruptions. Tears solved nothing. "Naomi said it's easier to say deep, scary things if I don't have to look you in the eye."

"You can try it. If you don't like it, stop."

"I told you my father cheated," I blurted. I wrapped my arms tighter around my middle, hugging Cormac's soft blankets close. His scent wafted around me, but still my body shook. Not from the cold—this was a visceral reaction, one I didn't fully understand. "Well, I didn't tell you all of that story. He went to work, like he always did, kissing my mother and me goodbye." I tipped my head back and stared at the ceiling. "She was a stay-at-home mom then. She'd taken some classes at the community college, but they had me young. My dad was in sales. He made good money…" I swallowed, hating this next part—the part that still left me feeling worthless. "After lunch, someone knocked on the door. A lawyer, delivering divorce papers. My dad wanted us out of the house. He…he had another family he planned to move into it."

Cormac made a sound in the back of his throat, but I refused to acknowledge it, him. I'd break if I did. I was alone in the dark, reciting my past. If I considered more, I'd want to end the call and curl into a ball.

"He didn't want to give us anything," I continued after a moment. "I wasn't supposed to know, but my mom wasn't good at hiding stuff. He told her she'd gotten pregnant on purpose, and that it had been a mistake to keep me." I let my lips drift upward, but it wasn't a smile. "And he said she'd delayed some of my development—giving him a dumb, useless kid to trap him."

"I want to hug you right now," Cormac said. "Help you through this."

"You can't. Just…listen, please. I don't think I can do this again." I rushed on. "The judge made my dad pay child support, but it was the bare minimum, and he always said he hated 'taking away from his proper family'. Even the judge agreed I shouldn't have anything to do with him after that outburst."

"He said that in front of you?" Anger laced Cormac's tone.

"Yes." Words I didn't want to repeat—words I didn't want in my head, even now.

"Your father's garbage."

"No arguments here."

Releasing a harsh breath as my shoulders drained of tension, I blinked back tears. With more effort, I slowed my breathing, calmed my racing pulse.

"I don't know what to say." His voice was softer.

"Maybe there's nothing to say."

"Oh, there's something. I'm just not sure what yet. Does he still live in Houston?"

"Yeah."

"Have you seen him?"

I scowled. "No, and I don't want to. My mother either. She, ah, she told me my motor-skill struggles pushed my dad over the edge, and that's why he left her. I haven't seen her since I left for college."

"I don't blame you."

The silence stretched out again. Then I heard the ring for a video call. I licked my lips, pulse pounding in my neck. Before I could second-guess myself, I pressed *Accept*.

Cormac's face filled the screen. He leaned against the headboard, one arm behind his neck, pillows supporting him.

"Keelie—wait, why are you in the dark?"

"It seemed an appropriate place to share the most terrible moments of my life, when I learned how unlovable I was."

He squinted, bringing his phone a little closer. With a sigh, his expression softened. "You are not unlovable."

I sniffled. "I feel that way."

His expression turned even more earnest. "You need to know something, and I want you to see my face when I say it: your feelings matter to me. *You* matter to me. I want you to be happy. Deliriously so."

I turned on my side, propping my phone on the neighboring pillow. "My parents...that's why trust is hard for me."

He nodded, expression sad. "I understand that much better now. So, here's what I can do: I'll always tell you my truth."

I smiled again, liking that he said *his* truth. That probably wouldn't always align with the happenings around him—something I hadn't understood until meeting him. But we all had things that colored our perceptions; my father's abandonment, his betrayal, and my mother's continual chasing of security had tainted my ability to see truth.

"I'll give you my truth, too," I promised.

Cormac nodded. "Here's the number-one truth I have where you're concerned: I'm falling in love with you."

CHAPTER 43
Cormac

She licked her lips, eyes wide. "I…"

"Don't feel like you need to say it back. I told you because you need to know." I frowned. "Though I'd planned this to be a lot more romantic."

She smiled, and it was shy. "It was kind of romantic." Her voice was soft. "I'm falling for you, Cormac. Hard. You're just too good—"

"Don't you dare say to be true. I'm me, you're you, and I love you."

Her smile grew. "I lo—"

"Please don't say it now." I groaned. "I want to kiss you." My dick twitched. "And worship your body like you deserve when you say it."

"O-okay."

I swallowed, trying to get my lust reined in enough that I could think. "Talk to me, please."

She blew out a breath, and I watched her snuggle deeper into my pillows. Fucking perfection. The only thing better would be if I were there with her, holding her.

"I want to hear all about your day," she said. "And don't leave out any of the details about how awesome it was to scoot around Dukovsky and score."

I grinned. "That's a good place to start."

I smiled, pleased by Keelie's deep, even breaths. Her phone remained propped up on the neighboring pillow, her features invisible thanks to the shadows of the room. Still, I touched the glass over the curve of her cheek. I wanted nothing more than to kiss her temple and have her snuggle into my chest. And to fuck her long and hard so she knew she was mine, just as I was hers.

I scrubbed my hand over my face, blinking to hold back the emotions flooding me. "You hold my heart, pretty girl."

"Cormac? Miss you. So much," she murmured. She flipped over, curling deeper into her pillow.

No wonder Keelie had gone into occupational therapy. She was trying to save all the kids like her from the pain and abandonment, the betrayal of trust she'd lived through. She was so much stronger than she gave herself credit for. But she was also terrified to let herself love.

I ended the call, hoping the change in light didn't wake her. But I didn't want her to awaken to a dead phone.

I needed to make sure she knew how much she meant to me, so I opened my web browser and found a florist that would deliver to her school.

I rose, stretched, and strode to the bathroom. Ablutions complete, I crawled into the bed. Keelie needed to be wooed. She needed to feel safe. Only then would she let herself love me like I loved her. Fully. With abandon.

I'd never planned to love another woman, yet there she was, deep in my heart.

Good thing I knew Naomi, Adam, Maxim, and the rest of the team would be more than happy to help me win Keelie over.

"It wasn't this hard back in high school."

"What's that?"

Cruz stood in the doorway, weaving a little. I disliked the room-sharing policy, but rooming with Cruz wasn't too bad. He was a grumpy bastard who rarely hooked up. He believed he frightened women. And he didn't snore, so I didn't complain about rooming with him.

I shook my head. "Nothing. I was just thinking that my last attempt at romancing a woman was easier."

He shut the door and tripped his way toward his bed. "Drank too many damn beers," he moaned. "What was the rookie thinking?"

"That he's nineteen and loves the Canadian drinking age?"

"Stupid kid's going to be dragging his ass tomorrow," Cruz grumbled.

I chuckled. "So are you."

Cruz slid under the covers, evidently too tired to change his clothes. "Women haven't changed in fifteen years," he muttered.

"What's that?"

"Women. They still want to feel loved, be appreciated. They like knowing you're thinking about them. Same things we want."

"Huh. Good advice."

But Cruz was asleep. I reached over and flicked off the light.

CHAPTER 44
Keelie

"Ms. Hayes, could you please come to the office?" Lorraine, the school secretary, called through the speaker.

"I'll be there after I finish with my student. About ten minutes."

"All right. See you then."

Concern tinged my thoughts as I finished up with Andy, but I pushed it back. By the time I walked toward the office, though, worry had settled in. What if a parent was angry with me? What if something happened to Ida Jane? What if the Wildcatters' plane had crashed? My thoughts spun, each possibility more terrible than the last.

When I entered, there was an enormous bouquet on the desk, with my friend Lisa and two other teachers cooing over the arrangement. The blooms were all soft pinks and purples with some darker red accents.

"Wow," I said. "Someone's feeling loved." I peered around the arrangement at Lorraine, whose smile widened. "What's up?"

"Well, those are for you." She nodded at the flowers.

My jaw dropped. "What?"

"And...there's a note!" She half rose from her chair to point at the small white envelope. Two of the teachers stepped back, eying me speculatively, but Lisa came closer, her eyes twinkling.

My cheeks burned even as a smile bloomed along with my blush. I plucked the card and opened the envelope. My hands trembled as I read the note: *You brighten my day and my life so much. I hope these do the same for you. Love, Cormac*

My smile widened.

"Ah…" Lisa jumped up and down, holding her photocopies to her chest. "Keelie's got a hot hockey player boyfriend."

"We know," Lorraine said. "He was here on campus a couple of weeks ago, with his very attractive friend." She fanned her cheeks.

"What's going on?" Ms. Schein, the principal, appeared in her doorway, tugging down her glasses. She noted the flowers, me clutching the note, and the avid faces. "Mmm… Young love, I take it." A no-nonsense administrator with over twenty years of experience, she kept her steel gray hair short and tucked behind her ears. But her eyes danced with humor, accented by the laugh lines around her mouth.

"Correct," Lorraine announced. "Keelie's dating Cormac Bouchard."

Mrs. Schein raised an eyebrow. "That won't impede your work, will it?"

I shook my head. "No, ma'am."

"Good. The kids need to be the top priority during your work hours."

"Of course."

Mrs. Schein stepped forward—none of us could resist the beautiful blooms. "If he wanted to talk to the kids about moving their bodies, sports, nutrition, how to set goals, anything, I'm sure we could find a time for an assembly."

I pulled out one of the lavender hydrangeas and handed it to her. "I'll talk to him."

She winked. "Do that. And I'm open to any other ideas he might have to engage the children." With a nod, she turned and went back to her office, her nose pressed into the soft petals.

"You got Sergeant Schein's approval," Lorraine whispered, eyes wide.

"I guess I did. Mind if I leave these with you in here until the end of the day?" I touched a velvety-soft lily.

"Not at all. I'll keep them safe," Lorraine said.

My phone rang as I settled my beautiful flowers on Cormac's kitchen table. Ida Jane would be home soon. We'd planned to swim and then eat one of Cormac's chef-made dinners.

Naomi and Nicole were correct that there were some serious perks to dating professional athletes. With a long, heartfelt sigh, I admitted that I wanted *Cormac* whispering love in my ear as he pressed me into his bed and made me his.

Then maybe I would believe he wanted *me*.

I touched the flowers again and smiled—until I looked at my phone and saw my mother's number. I declined the call, my good mood souring.

My mother called again. Then again.

"Hello?" I finally answered.

"Your father's going to be calling. He wants to talk to you."

"Well, I don't want to talk to him."

She grunted. "I don't either, but we don't always get what we want."

My scowl deepened. "You gave him my number."

"He's your father, Keelie."

Somehow, my mother saw me as the one thing holding our family together, whereas I wanted nothing more than to forget my father existed.

I clenched my teeth. My phone beeped, telling me I had another call. "I have to go."

I pressed my fingertips to my forehead, over the spot where a deep ache had developed.

"Hi."

"What's wrong?" Cormac asked. "You sound sad."

"Nothing. The flowers are beautiful."

"They were too much. Dammit. I didn't mean—"

"No, they're beautiful. Perfect. They made all of us smile. Thank you."

"Then, what's wrong?"

"Did you arrive in Edmonton all right?" I asked.

"Yes, we finished practice, and the guys are deciding where they want to eat. Keelie, what's wrong?"

"My father." My voice cracked. "After twenty-one years, suddenly he wants to talk to me. Probably because my name's linked to yours." My tone brewed bitterness, and the ache spread, pounding against my skull.

"That worthless piece of..." Cormac bit back the curse.

"Yeah." My shoulders dropped. "He is."

"Do you think he'll bother you?"

I considered the question. "Yes."

Cormac growled. "Will you let me take care of it?"

I nibbled my lip. My initial reaction was to tell him no; I'd handle my father. But couples worked through problems together. I took a deep breath, wishing I could calm my racing pulse. "We can come up with a plan together." The words rushed out of me.

"Yeah, we could do that. But I don't want you meeting him or even talking to him before I get back," Cormac said.

"Okay."

"Keelie?"

"Yeah?"

"I love you."

I smiled as worry about my father slid away. Cormac loved me. I could handle anything.

CHAPTER 45
Cormac

I paused, balanced on the threshold between my garage and laundry room, shocked by the cascade of laughter pouring from the living room.

"Stop," Keelie gasp-squealed. "Oh my Go—stop it!"

I hurried through the kitchen, my heart hammering, only to stop again as I caught sight of Keelie, bent over, holding her waist, face red with mirth. Ida Jane raised a microphone to her lips and began singing "Sweet Caroline" with the help of the microphone's karaoke feature. The notes were tinny, and she changed the name to Keelie-Mine.

My grin grew until my cheeks hurt. I'd missed this. *Connection. Laughter.* Keelie raised her head, and her eyes found mine with unerring accuracy: *Love.*

Damn, how I loved her.

She brought joy into my world. This was the first time I'd walked through my door to anything other than sterile cleanliness—everything just as I left it. This mess made my house a home—fallen throw pillows, cat fur on my rugs, a hoodie tossed over the back of my couch, and snack bowls and drinks on the coffee table. I'd missed that without even realizing it.

Keelie rose to her full height as I strode forward. We met next to my leather sofa as Ida Jane quit singing, lowering the microphone. I cupped Keelie's cheek, fingers sinking into her hair and lips, claiming hers as she slid her cool palm up my nape and rose on tiptoe to meet me.

The kiss exploded with yearning, heat, and love. I tilted my head, delving deeper into her warm, sweet mouth. She tasted like caramel corn.

"Wow. That's some greeting," I could vaguely hear Ida Jane mumble. "Erm, well, I can see you and Keelie have some unfinished business, so I'll just skedaddle."

"You're not running away again," Maxim rumbled from the kitchen. He must have stopped there, no doubt entranced by Ida Jane's clear, strong soprano.

I lifted my head and smiled at Keelie, dropping another brief kiss on her sweet lips. "Missed you, pretty girl."

She snuggled against me, and my body responded. She raised her eyebrows. "I can tell. I missed you, too. So much."

I chuckled as I dropped my hands to her hips, enjoying the soft give in her belly against my straining zipper. I nipped at her ear but said nothing because Maxim and Ida Jane were arguing.

"Those two have fireworks," Keelie murmured, glancing over my shoulder.

"Not as many as us."

She giggled but moved around me, leaving my arms empty, my chest cooling. I wanted to snatch her back, but she seemed to need to stand next to her friend.

"Of course I came to collect you. I told you I would," Maxim said. Exasperation sat on his features, his styled hair now mussed.

"I was havin' fun with Keelie."

"You can have fun with me."

"Not the same kind," she shot back.

Maxim growled. "Better kind."

At Keelie's tense glance, I stepped forward. "Coach decided we should fly back for an extra practice tomorrow morning. Our second line turned out a sloppy performance, and he's not taking chances now that we're getting close to the playoffs."

"The win tonight was great," Keelie said, shuffling until she once again rested against my chest.

"It would have been better if Naese had held his position," Maxim said. He motioned to Ida Jane. "We should go."

She crossed her arms over her chest. "Maybe I wanna stay here."

"And hear them?" Maxim gestured toward me. Keelie gasped, her cheeks turning cherry red. Ida Jane flicked an uncertain glance our way.

"You saw how they went at it—and that was in public. Wait till they get to their bedroom."

Keelie quivered beside me. I slipped my arm around her, leaning down to whisper, "I want to smell you on my sheets. I want to do many, many things to you in my bed tonight."

"See? You don't want to stay here. My house will be quiet and secure. You can get a good night's sleep before your big presentation tomorrow."

Ida Jane let Maxim tow her away, but she asked, "How do you know about my presentation? Were you snooping through my emails again? Maxim, that's too far. You can't just…"

Her voice trailed away as they walked up the stairs, no doubt to collect her bags.

I swung Keelie back into my arms, bracing one forearm along her spine. I rained kisses along her jaw. "Damn, being away from you is hard," I murmured.

"But I like you coming back."

Her hips shifted, restless, as her hands gripped my shirt. She tipped her head back, giving me access to her throat.

"I missed you, too," she moaned as I slid my tongue along the sensitive skin. When I pulled back, her face beamed with happiness that made my heart ache. "I want to show you how much."

"You don't have to—"

She rose to her toes and wound her arms around my neck. Her lips brushed mine, featherlight and unsatisfying. My fingers flexed against the taut skin of her hips and sweet ass.

"I want to. I want you," she murmured against my lips. "Make me yours."

CHAPTER 46
Keelie

Cormac's eyes flared so hot my skin tingled, and I liked that feeling.

"You already are mine, but yes, baby. I'll fuck you so good; you'll have no doubts who you belong to. Who *I* belong to."

He swept me into his arms, the thick, steely muscles carrying me with ease. I ran my palms up and down his pecs, around his neck, and into his hair as I peppered his chin, cheeks, and lips with kisses.

He groaned as we hit the stairs, the sound resonating from deep in his chest. "Keelie, this craving for you—"

"It's all-consuming."

"Huge."

"So don't wait any longer. I want you, too." I blushed harder than ever, still unable to say aloud that I wanted Cormac to fuck me. Those weren't words I said because I worried I wouldn't be able to censor myself with the kids if I started. Still, I loved the naughty shiver and pulse of heat I felt each time Cormac talked dirty.

Instead of setting me on my feet next to the bed, he bent, depositing me on the mattress, the coolness of the comforter too much against my heated skin. I arched upward, away from the chill just as Cormac brought his large, aroused body down over mine.

"Yes. That's perfect. Show me how much you want me."

I wrapped my legs around his waist, cradling his large erection right where I needed it—in the V of my splayed thighs. He tilted his hips, pressing tighter against me, the friction causing my pulse to race and my hips to roll.

"Keelie." He drew out the word. "You feel so good. So warm and welcoming. Perfect."

I forced my eyes open and met his hungry stare. The way Cormac spoke to me, knowing that only I heard those words from his lips, made the moment more intimate. I kissed him, slipping my tongue into his mouth, trying to make him as crazed with passion as he made me.

Our tongues tangled and joined, the dance more sinuous than our bodies sliding against one another.

I broke away, gasping. Cormac removed my top and bra with an easy flick of his wrist. His hands moved over my breasts, thumb and forefingers tugging and twisting my nipples, which caused my hips to follow the same pattern as I cried out. Need bubbled up hotter, more pressing. Cormac kissed my neck, shoulder, and upper chest before his lips closed around my pebbled bud. I clasped his head to my chest, breath sawing from my lungs in an unintelligible cry as he suckled and nibbled, licked, and teased my sensitive flesh.

"More," I moaned.

He switched to the other breast, bathing it with the same attention. My panties were soaked. My hips thrust against his, and I scored his back, my nails catching on the cotton of his dress shirt.

"T-too many clothes," I gasped.

Each tug of his lips, each swirl of his tongue slammed into the needy ball in my core. He rose, his hips slipping away from mine. I cried out, frustrated at the loss of heat and friction. He tugged off my pants and panties, his lips still on my breast. I tried to unbutton his shirt but gave up, not wanting to disturb his work. I slid my hands down his sides and found his belt, which I undid with clumsy fingers. Leaving it hanging, I undid the button and slid down his zipper to cup his hot, hard cock.

He growled, nipping at the underside of my breast. "Keep doing that, and I won't make it inside you."

"Inside me," I said with an eager shimmy. "Now." I caught the waistband of his underwear—boxer briefs that hugged the taut muscles of his ass to splendid relief—and gripped that thick muscle, tugging him back between my splayed thighs.

He slipped to the side before he made contact, causing me to gnash my teeth in frustration. "Cormac!"

"Shh, pretty girl. I got you. I'm going to make this so good for you."

"It already is. Please." I slammed my right foot into the comforter, tears building.

He pressed tighter to my left side, his thick fingers slipping up my damp thigh to my achy core. Without hesitation, he slipped two fingers inside me. I bucked my hips, and he groaned.

"So wet. So hot. So perfect." He pressed his other hand to my belly, thumb rubbing soothing half circles as he held me to the bed. He pulled his fingers out and pushed them back in over and over as I focused on the sensation.

"I want…" I couldn't finish the thought.

My thighs shivered as I tried to raise my hips. He thrust another finger inside me, opening me even more, before curling those fingers against my front wall…and hitting that magical spot that caused me to detonate.

I screamed, my hands tugging at my hair, my body desperate to twist closer even as I wanted to shy away from the pleasure overwhelming me. Cormac held me down as he worked me through the climax, which went on and on.

The convulsions finally eased, and he kissed my forehead, right along the edge of my sweat-soaked hairline.

"That was beautiful."

The proud angles of his face were tight with desire. Reflected in his eyes, I saw my sprawled body there, open to him. I cupped his cheek. "Put on that condom." I nodded toward his bedside table. "I want you inside me."

"Keelie." He closed his eyes. When they opened, he appeared more serious than I'd ever seen him. "If I'm inside you, it's going to mean everything to me. You understand? I don't want you for now. I want you forever. Here. With me."

I brushed his soft hair back from his brow. "I understand."

"You're sure? I'm going to make you mine." His hips thrust restlessly, as if the mere thought of being with me, being mine, just as I was his, made him crazy.

"Yes. I want you." A spark of feminine power burned in my chest as I licked my lips. I rolled on top of him. And this time, when I reached for the drawer, I pulled out that fresh box of condoms. I opened the box, my fingers fumbling as my hands shook with need. He took the packet from me. Once he'd ripped it open, he rolled it down his impressive length, all while I tried not to hyperventilate. I was about to have sex with Cormac Bouchard.

He wanted me.

Me.

He gripped my hips and, with a needy sound, thrust upward toward my warm, wet heat. I rubbed against him, loving how his hot flesh split my lips, making me ache for him.

"I love you, Cormac."

He growled and kissed me, his tongue tangling with mine.

"I love you," he breathed against my lips.

I tried to look stern, but his cock teasing my inner lips made it hard. "I'm all in with you."

"All in," he groaned.

"No one else—"

"You're all I think about, the only woman I see."

Happiness blossomed at his words as much as the unhinged gleam in his eye. I lifted and sank down over the silky hardness, taking him deep inside me with a single move.

We both stilled, breath held, gazes locked. He pulsed inside me, and my tender muscles clenched back.

This was a new dance, even better than our mouths, but I dropped my head so our tongues, too, could dance.

He shifted and thrust up inside me. Hard. Out, in. I whimpered. He did it again, and again, pounding into my body, his hands clasping my waist, his mouth and tongue owning me just as much as his cock did.

I clung to his shirt, unable to do more as sensations blasted me. He flipped us over so I lay beneath him, and he sank into me again. We both moaned at the new friction.

He yanked his mouth from mine, and his beautiful erection slipped from me. I cried out, shocked and desperate for more.

"Just getting undressed," he panted. "Need to feel...skin to skin. Much as I can."

I shuddered, wondering what he'd feel like inside me with no barriers. Buttons flew, one sailing past my cheek. He did that sexy one-hand pull over his head, yanking off his undershirt as he kicked away his shoes and pants. Then, hundreds of pounds of aroused male settled over me. My nipples puckered even harder as his chest brushed against them. And he slammed back inside me, the hot, hard silk of his erection spreading my lips and pounding into my body.

I should have known that Cormac, a professional athlete built for stamina and power, would fuck me better and harder than anyone else ever could. The fourth orgasm slid over me, and I cried out, weakly this time, as he continued to snap his hips in and out.

I shuddered, my legs and arms limp from pleasure. He grasped my hips and tilted them up while he settled on his knees, my ass on his thighs, and drove home, once, twice... The third time, his head fell back, his lips parted, and he groaned as he spurted deep inside me. His erection jerked, filling the condom with his cum.

Then he collapsed beside me, reached for me, and tucked me against his warm, powerful body.

CHAPTER 47
Cormac

I tried to catch my breath. I couldn't. My head spun from the power of my release, even as my muscles turned lethargic.

That hadn't been a normal orgasm. That was a full-body experience. My glutes ached, my abs tingled, and my dick was ecstatic. I kissed Keelie's forehead and left my nose against her fanned-out hair, drinking in this moment. Because it was special. Beautiful. Worth savoring.

I wanted to remember it forever.

She turned, and the silky strands of her hair tugged against my cheek. I should have lifted my head, but contentment and exhaustion pulled at me, keeping me down. She wrapped her arms around me and snuggled closer.

I opened one eye to find her regarding me. Uncertainty slithered across her features, and that caused me to tighten my hold.

"I've never felt something like that before," I told her.

Her body relaxed against mine. "Me neither. I wondered…"

I raised an eyebrow. She blushed so hot that my forearm heated where our skin touched. She cleared her throat. "I wondered if it was always like that. For you."

My heart cracked a little. This woman. She was so brave, so beautiful, and yes, a little broken. I never wanted her to feel timid with me.

"No, pretty girl. What we just did was…" I considered, trying to find the right word. "Transcendent," I decided. I punctuated my statement with a nod. My breathing had evened out, and my body felt loose, good—no, great. Better than it had in years.

She bit her lip, so I tugged the soft, pink flesh from her teeth and licked it with all the gentleness I could muster.

"That was the most special experience of my life." She dropped her lashes so I could no longer see those sparkling eyes. "I love you, Cormac. More than anyone else. Ever."

I gathered her closer and pressed another kiss to her temple. "I love you, too, pretty girl."

CHAPTER 48
Keelie

As the next few weeks unfolded, I felt like I was living in a princess fantasy. I went to all of Cormac's home games and joined the ladies at Naomi's for the away games. Ida Jane and I talked multiple times each week, and she stayed with me at Cormac's house when the team traveled.

Cormac picked me up from work whenever he could, and he took me for more golf lessons. We swam in his pool and made out in his sauna as often as possible.

Like right now. His lips slid down my damp neck, nipping at my pounding pulse as the dry heat swirled around us.

"Cormac," I groaned.

"I love the way you say my name."

"C-Cormac," I whispered, thrilled when desire flared between us.

"I want us hot, sweaty, and naked in bed," he said. He picked me up and carried me from the sauna. I shivered when the cool air hit my skin and clasped my arms tighter around his neck, resting my heated cheek against his shoulder.

I heard my phone ring from where we'd left them outside the sauna, and I tensed. I knew who that was: my father. His attempts to contact me had ramped up. I hadn't told Cormac how often my father was calling and texting, not wanting anything to ruin our pleasant day-to-day existence.

"What is it?" Cormac asked, slowing his stride.

"I'm sure it's nothing." I tangled my fingers in the short hair at the nape of his neck as I pressed kisses to his collarbone. "Take me upstairs."

He switched directions and settled on one of his barstools. "I will, but first, you need to talk to me." I remained wrapped in his arms, safe.

I clenched my eyes shut. "It may be nothing…"

"Keelie."

I sighed. "My father's been calling and texting. A lot."

Cormac raised an eyebrow. "You said it wasn't bad."

I had said that. Twisting my hands together, I said, "I'm…I'm managing him."

Cormac lifted me and plopped me in the seat next to him. I bit back a whimper. I needed him right now. Rising from his chair, he walked to the fridge. He poured us both some of his freshly-squeezed grapefruit juice and divided a can of lime seltzer between the two glasses. He brought them over and set one in front of me.

"I don't want you to deal with him alone," Cormac said, his tone steady. "I want to help you sort this out."

I took a long swig of my drink. "He's still embarrassed that we're related. I don't want you to hear what he says."

Cormac's jaw clenched. "Well, now I'm even more determined to talk to him." He rose and stepped in closer, towering over me. "Especially if he's belittling you."

"It's my problem."

"It's *our* problem."

I shrank smaller. Cormac eased his arms on either side of me and nuzzled into my hair. "Let me in, Keelie. Dammit. I need you to let me in."

Flinging my head back, I met his gaze. "I have. I *did*. I told you I love you—I practically live here—"

"Make it official," he said.

"W-what?"

"Move in with me. Live here. You and Slippers."

I gawked.

"I don't think you get how much it comforts me to know you're here, sleeping in my bed. That you're safe, especially now that I know your father's harassing you." His jaw flexed.

He wouldn't let that go. I sucked in a breath, my heart pounding. The sauna might have left me lightheaded, but the turn this conversation had taken caused my confusion. *Move in?* Hand over my problems?

Then I'd become my mother. She'd never learned how to live on her own. To this day, she was still bitter and poor. I'd found pictures of her before my dad left, and she was a completely different woman—her hair and eyes shone and her smile was wide.

When my dad betrayed her, divorced her, he took away her security and her happiness. I shuddered. I remembered what he'd said then, and it wasn't much different from what he told me now. If Cormac heard those horrible things, he might believe them, and then...

I'd *be* my mother. Heartbroken. Alone.

"I..." I sucked in a breath and lifted my chin. "I'll deal with my father."

Cormac slammed his hand against the counter, causing me to yelp. "Dammit! Why won't you let me help you?"

"Be-because then I'm like her," I replied.

He stepped back. "Like who?"

"My mother."

He scowled. "*How* could you be like her? You have a master's degree in a sought-after field. You have a house and a retirement account, which is more than your mom does."

My eyes widened. He was right. But I couldn't stop the panic building within me. I stood, the barstool scraping across the wood. "I don't want to talk about this. I want to get dressed."

"Well, I want to handle this so you're not flinching every time your phone rings."

"You can't solve everything, Cormac. This is *my* issue, and *I'll* deal with it my way."

His jaw jutted as he stepped back. "Fine. But don't keep secrets from me, Keelie." He turned on his heel and walked toward the stairs. "I'm going to change and head to the gym. I need some time alone."

I twisted my fingers together, my chest aching. I still stood there when Cormac came back down the stairs in athletic shorts and a T-shirt. He gave me a fiery glare that caused me to flinch before he disappeared down the hallway.

My phone chimed again, and I sucked in a breath. Raising my chin, I reminded myself I wasn't my mother. I *wouldn't* be her. With trembling fingers, I pulled my phone from my purse and opened the texts.

As I'd expected, the message was from my father. *Stop ignoring me. It just makes you look weak and pathetic. What could a man as powerful as Cormac see in you?*

I swallowed with difficulty, the words blurring on the screen. This was what I never wanted him to see. Just like I didn't want Cormac to know how much those words hurt me—how correct my father was.

I glanced longingly down the hall. I should have just shown him. Then he would have stayed.

CHAPTER 49
Cormac

My phone chimed, but I ignored it, focusing on my breathing as I completed another set with the weights. Arms burning, I grunted as I set them down. Then I swiped a towel across my sweaty face and neck and pulled out my phone.

My stomach burned as I noted Keelie's name.

I opened the message, irritated that she hadn't come in to talk to me.

Don't contact me again. You mean nothing to me. Cormac doesn't want to meet you or talk to you either.

Below that message were multiple others she'd copied from who I assumed was her father. I clenched my jaw as words popped out at me: *pathetic, weak, stupid, not good enough.* This man was scum. Who talked to a woman, his child—any person—like that?

My heart sank. Keelie's expression and her reluctance to share this made more sense now. She'd been struggling with abuse, and I'd yelled at her.

"Fuck," I shouted as I threw my towel across the room. I took a long breath in, released it. Again, I did that. I knew now what I was dealing with… I hoped I could fix this.

No, I would fix this. Starting now.

I sat my ass down on the weight bench and got to work.

The first thing was the easiest: I bought Keelie a new phone. I asked to have it set up on her current account, but her father wouldn't have this contact information.

The next step was fun: I started ring shopping. But I soon realized I wanted to do that in person, so I switched gears to the last item on my list. I composed a message to my parents, informing them that I planned to ask Keelie to marry me.

Keelie was asleep when I made my way upstairs a few hours later. The light was on in the bathroom and the door partially open so I could see. Slippers was curled up next to Keelie, who had her arm around the cat. Tear tracks streaked her cheeks.

"Oh, sweetheart." I settled my hip next to hers. Part of me wanted to let her sleep, but we needed to talk. I left for another away game tomorrow. If I'd had the time, I would have talked to her first and implemented my plan later, but I needed to know Keelie was safe.

"Cormac?" she murmured.

"I'm here, Keelie. I'm right here with you. I'm sorry I yelled. I wasn't mad at you." I swallowed hard. "That was about me—my insecurities."

"I'm scared you're going to leave me." She choked on a sob. "I don't want to be like my mother. I don't want to be weak and stupid and—"

"You're not." I pulled her up into my arms. Slippers hissed and darted off the bed. I'd have to make it up to her later.

"You're so smart and capable and beautiful." I pressed kisses to her temples, cheeks, lips. "I love you. Just the way you are. I love you, Keelie."

She wrapped her arms around me so tightly I nearly suffocated, and she sobbed. "I want him to go away. I w-was h-h-happy."

I stroked her hair and her back. "Being with you makes me happy."

"He w-w-won't stop."

She cried, and it broke my heart. I wanted to cry, too, and my head ached. I clenched my jaw and held her, trying to soothe her.

Spent, she rested her cheek against my shoulder. "I'm sorry I keep messing up your life."

"Look at me."

When she did, her eyes were red-rimmed and bloodshot. Her nose and cheeks were blotchy.

"You make my life better," I told her. "I need you to understand that. Your father's a nuisance. Well, more like a total asshole. But *we'll* deal with him. Okay? We're going to start with a new phone and a number he doesn't have."

She studied me for a long time before she nodded. Her breath puffed against my neck. "Okay."

"I love you, Keelie."

She lifted her hand and cupped my cheek. "I love you, Cormac. So much."

CHAPTER 50
Keelie

The next morning, I woke up in Cormac's bed. I smiled as I stretched, languorous, as Cormac kissed his way down my belly. He glanced up, his expression filled with heat.

"Lift your hips."

When I did, he slipped my panties off as he raked his teeth across my hipbones. I closed my eyes as he continued the slow path downward.

"I love you, Keelie," he murmured. He kissed each inner thigh, flicking his tongue against the sensitive skin.

"Cormac!"

"Tell me you love me. I need to hear you say it."

"I love you."

"And you won't keep secrets?"

"I won't. I promise." My voice broke as he nipped the sensitive skin of my inner thigh.

Pleasure receded as my mind processed what he'd said. Oh. *Oh.* Cormac had mentioned his own demons. Shannon must have made him feel as if he wasn't enough—good enough for her world. I wriggled out from under him and molded my body to his. My arms wound around his neck, and I kissed him, pouring all my love, all my devotion into the kiss.

He stared at me. "I need to help you."

I relaxed. "Okay."

"I need you to talk to me when you're scared or worried."

I nodded.

"And…"

I held my breath. He was going to ask me to move in again. I wanted him to. I wanted to say yes.

"I need to make you come before you go to work."

Work was a challenge because my father would not stop texting me. I wanted that new phone, but Cormac was busy. It would come in time. I turned off my ringer, but that meant I missed messages from Cormac and Ida Jane. Frustrated, I slammed my way into Cormac's house…and found Ida Jane standing in the kitchen, mouth agape.

"You're in a foul mood."

"I am."

"Well, your boyfriend wants you to call him."

"He's got a game tonight."

She crossed her arms and raised an eyebrow. "That man will make time for you."

"Fine." I picked up my phone, but Ida Jane snatched it from my hand.

"With this one." She plopped a brand-new phone into my hand with a smile. I turned it over, noting the Wildcatters logo and Cormac's number. The home screen said, "Keelie's phone."

"He bought me a new phone already?" I asked, my heart pattering in a sweet rhythm.

"With a new number. All your contacts are in it, but your dad can't bug you." She smiled. "Dad problem solved."

I slouched onto one of the barstools. "Cormac asked me to move in while we were in the middle of a heated discussion." Slippers jumped up into my lap, and I scratched her chin. The cat seemed to note my half-hearted attempts at loving her and lost interest, heading toward her food bowl, tail straight up in the air.

"Okay," Ida Jane said, voice cautious.

"He hasn't brought it up again." I licked my lips. "What if he changed his mind?"

"Then you talk to him and sort it out."

I lifted my brows. "Like you do with Maxim."

She scowled. "There's no *talking* to that brute."

My new phone rang, causing me to jump. I smiled as George Strait began belting out "I Cross My Heart."

"Hello?"

"Good. You have your new phone," Cormac said, tone brisk.

"Thank you."

"You're welcome. I wanted to let you know that I spoke with Coach and some of the staff. We think the best course of action against your father is a restraining order. If that doesn't make him stop bothering you, I'll get my lawyer involved."

"Cormac…" I swallowed the ball of emotion. I noted that Ida Jane had disappeared. "Thank you."

"No thanks necessary. What do I keep telling you?" he said, his voice soft.

"That I matter, and you want me happy."

"That's right, but you forgot one very important thing—Shit! I have to go. Skate time. I'll call you after we get to the hotel."

"Bye," I whispered, but he was already gone.

I powered down my old phone with a sigh of relief. Such a weight lifted not having to view those messages. I got up and made myself a grapefruit spritzer, my new favorite drink. I pulled out the dinner Cormac had had his chef leave for Ida Jane and me. Everything he did showed his love. So why couldn't I show him I was just as committed to us—and to our future?

CHAPTER 51
Cormac

The next day, I arrived back in Houston after a brutal loss to the Avalanche. Nik and Naese were both limping, thanks to some dirty high-sticking, and Cruz's hand was taped because of a broken ring finger. On the plus side, Ida Jane had promised to help me shop for the perfect ring.

"You can't take my girl ring shopping," Maxim snarled when I told him the plan. We were still seated on the plane, waiting for the jet bridge so we could exit.

"I'm not buying *Ida Jane* a ring; I'm buying one for Keelie."

Maxim had been angry since we left. Based on how he'd just tried to rip my head off, he and Ida Jane weren't getting along. I wondered if they'd be able to work out whatever their issue was, but I didn't ask—Maxim wouldn't tell me until he was ready.

"I'll go with you," he said. "The two of you, I mean." He smiled, his eyes taking on a devious glint. "Then I'll know what Ida Jane likes when I'm ready to propose."

I shook my head and chuckled. "Whatever, man. It's just got to be discreet. I want this to be a surprise."

"All the more reason I should go," he said. "People will think I'm buying a ring for Ida Jane." He scowled. "Maybe that'll flush out her piece-of-shit ex."

I slapped his shoulder. "Solid plan. So, next week—Friday's

best, according to Ida Jane. After practice."

Eight days. Just over one week and I'd be able to complete my plan—and make sure Keelie understood how important she was to me.

"I'll make sure Ida Jane can meet us on her lunch break."

I grabbed my carry-on and deplaned, looking forward to seeing Keelie.

The moment I walked in the door at home, I clasped her to me. "Damn, I enjoy having you here," I said against her lips.

Hers curved upward. "I like it, too."

Asking her to move in was on the tip of my tongue, but I held off. No. I'd ask her to marry me first. Keelie needed to feel secure before she took the leap of giving up her house. I wouldn't ask her to move in again until she knew I meant forever.

While she put away her work materials and took a shower, I finished up dinner—the whitefish she enjoyed. We settled at the table, and I picked up her hand to kiss her knuckles. I looked forward to my ring living on her finger. Very, very much.

"How was school?" I asked.

"Good. Andy's making so much progress." Her smile turned bittersweet. "I don't think he'll need to be in my class next year."

"Is it hard when the kids move on?"

She nodded. "Yes, but it's tempered." She took a sip of her drink. "I mean, that's what's supposed to happen if I'm good at my job."

"I wish you could see yourself through my eyes," I said.

She glanced up with a shy smile. "I'm learning."

I rose from my seat and pulled her from hers, kissing her the way I wanted to. We ended up not eating dinner until later, but we were both okay with that.

Keelie came to our game the next evening, Thursday, and then the next day I had to get ready for another away game. I wished Ida Jane could take time off to look at rings before next Friday, but she was slammed with projects. I considered going by myself, but I needed the *perfect* ring. Nothing else would do. I had little time, anyway. We were scheduled to fly out this afternoon for our two-game series, first in Nashville on Saturday night, then Dallas on Sunday.

I'd left Keelie a message telling her our departure was going to be earlier than expected, so I wouldn't get to see her before we left. My doorbell rang just as a text popped up.

Forgot to tell you today was a half day! I'm on my way home. See you soon.

I smiled, glad I'd get to spend some time with Keelie before I left. Checking the video screen, I frowned when I saw Shannon at my front door. "Damn meddling mother," I mumbled. I didn't want Keelie to run into Shannon, but I also didn't want Shannon in my house. I muttered a curse, deciding my best course of action was to explain once and for all that I'd moved on.

I opened the door. "Shannon."

"Cormac. Thank goodness you're here. I really need to talk to you."

I ground my teeth together. "Does it matter that I have nothing to say?"

Her eyes pleaded with me. "Don't, Cormac. Please. We need

to talk. About…about us."

"I'm not interested in that. I've moved on. You need to leave."

I pulled out my phone and texted Maxim: *Get your ass over here. I need you to remove Shannon ASAP.*

She's there?

Yes. Hurry up!

"I'm trying to talk to you, Mac," Shannon snapped. "We need to discuss our marriage. Our future."

I lifted my head from my phone. "And I told you I'm not interested. We're divorced."

I didn't need her to lecture me about marriage. I'd poured my heart and soul into making her happy, but Shannon had thrown me away. Now that I was happy again, she assumed she could just step back into the role as my wife?

The sheer audacity of that thinking shouldn't have surprised me. Shannon planned to be a judge by thirty-five. But it did. Shock coated my mouth, making it dry.

"Immaturity caused our divorce," she continued in her lawyerly voice, the one I'd found so fucking hot when we were married. Not any more—just like I didn't find her unwillingness to listen to anything other than annoying.

"I know *exactly* why our marriage failed," I snapped. "And it wasn't immaturity. It was *your* infidelity. Now, again, I want you to leave."

Her jaw dropped and hurt crept into her expression. "We weren't married anymore. You can't claim—"

I squared my shoulders, realizing she wouldn't leave without having this out. Damn her timing. Damn my mother for pushing a narrative that was so fucking dead and buried; there wasn't even dust left.

"You'd sent me divorce papers, but I hadn't signed them. We were *not* divorced, Shannon."

She blinked up at me as if I'd just kicked her puppy. I gritted my teeth as the hurt gripped my throat. "He was and is one of the biggest douches I've ever met. You fucked him to make a point. It was received, and I won't ever forget."

She twisted her hands together. "But your mom said—"

"I don't give a shit what she said."

Shannon swallowed. "I still love you, Mac."

I shrugged. "That's unfortunate, because I don't love you."

That ship had sailed. And I wasn't interested in rehashing one of the biggest failures of my life. Except now, finally, I could see our marriage and subsequent divorce as necessary for my growth. Until then, everything had fallen into place—come too easily. And, yeah, that made me sound like an asshole. But I had been an asshole with too much talent and too much confidence. Having Coach Gauthier drop that career bomb on me blew up every entitled bone in my body. For the first time, after Gauthier traded me to Houston, I had to look at myself and dissect my decisions. And I came to realize I needed to develop resilience and learn to face adversity.

These past few years, I'd focused on being the best player, best captain, and best man I could be. I liked the guy who stared back at me in the mirror, something I couldn't have said a few years ago. And I'd learned to listen, to ponder, to consider others' opinions because I wasn't always right. I liked that, too.

"You don't—you can't mean that," Shannon said. "I messed up, Mac. I get that you're mad at me. You were ready to move forward before me. I was just so frightened of becoming your shadow, not even a whole person. I needed the space to find *me*."

She snatched my hand and held my fingers even as I tried to extricate myself from her. Her desperation reeked, turning my stomach. I wanted this over. I wanted Keelie here instead.

"We should start a family. I wasn't ready before. But…but…if this is what you need, I'll get pregnant. Now."

Unable to wrap my mind around her words, I simply stared. Six years ago, I would have given *anything* to hear her say that. Hell, three years ago, even as I healed from her screwing Dukovsky, I would have grabbed her with both arms and fucked a baby into her belly at that very moment. But I caught the desperation in the twist of her mouth, the skittishness of her gaze.

"You don't mean that," I said, my tone gentle.

"I do." She stepped forward and placed her hand on my chest, right over my heart. "I miss you. I miss *us*. We were so good together, so in love."

She slid her arms up my chest, over my shoulders. My muscles trembled at this—the familiarity of Shannon's scent, her touch. Before I even processed it, my hands dropped to her hips.

"Cormac?" Keelie's voice called. "I wanted to give you a proper sendoff…"

Her voice trailed away as she stepped into the entryway. Her eyes widened, first with shock. I threw Shannon's arms from me, causing her to squawk as she faltered backward.

Hurt flickered across Keelie's features followed by…nothing.

She shut down right before me, her face rearranging into a neutral expression as she stared at something over my shoulder.

"I guess you're already getting one," she said, her tone quiet. She hesitated for the briefest of moments before she turned on her heel and fled.

"Keelie," I called, racing after her. "It's not what it looks like…"

She whipped open the garage door and headed toward her car. "I *trusted* you."

I charged after her, but she made it to her car, where she slammed the door. I pressed my hands to the cool glass of her window as she started the ignition.

"Keelie, listen to me—"

I leaped back, her tires barely missing the toes of my sneakers. I gripped my hair, my elbows pressed together in front of my face as I watched her car speed out of my driveway. "Dammit," I yelled. "Shit. Shit. *Shit!*"

I dropped my hands to my knees and panted, but my heart continued to tumble and crack.

"Mac?" Shannon's hand rested on my shoulder, rubbing.

I whirled to face her. "Do you see what you've done? She's *gone.*"

"I hate that she found out about us getting back together like that, but now—"

"*There is no us,*" I screamed. I stepped back, hands fisted, chest heaving. "You threw us away."

"No, I didn't. I…I took a pause."

There was no way Shannon believed the garbage tumbling from her mouth, not even if my mother put the ideas in her head.

"I've been without you for years, Shannon! You left me because your career mattered more than my dream of kids and grandkids."

"That's not fair!" Indignation caused color to bloom across her sculpted cheekbones. She was beautiful, but...hard. Elegant and perfect and not the woman I wanted.

"Oh?" I raised my eyebrows. "So I misheard you all those years ago?"

"No, but I was young. I wanted my own career."

I closed my eyes for a moment. "Are you saying you'd be willing to move to Houston, to start over with your practice, build it up again? What if I get traded, eh? Are you going to want to go to another state, get licensed there? What does that do to your judicial aspirations?"

She opened her mouth, then snapped it shut. "You're thirty-one. You won't be playing much longer..."

I snorted, somewhere between offended and impressed with her selfish view of the world. "You're still thinking about you and *only* you. And for the record, I signed a new five-year contract. After my years as a player are over, I plan to coach. That's just like being a player. I may have to move to get a better position, go to a better team."

She blinked at me. "You...you're staying in hockey?"

"Always. I love it. It's my passion."

"But..." She sank down onto the steps, her legs giving out. "But you could come home. Raise our son. Take him to hockey practice, coach *his* team." She peered up at me, hope in her eyes.

"While you get your judgeship and rub elbows with judicial

scholars? Spend nights at soirees and talk with big words no one outside of your circle knows, let alone understands? No, I don't want that. I *never* wanted that."

She slumped further. "Oh my God...I *really* messed up." She scrubbed her hands over her face. "I planned it all out. I just assumed..."

I remained quiet, letting her process the absolute end of us.

"I'm sorry, Mac," Shannon said, her eyes filled with tears. "I...I didn't think about what you wanted or needed. Again. Maybe always. I'm so sorry."

I speared my fingers through my hair, which was longer now—I never cut it or my beard once we got this close to the playoffs. Sure, it was a superstition, but in my twelve years in the league, I'd had many more wins than losses. No reason to rock the boat.

"You're right, you didn't, and now Keelie's hurt. She's freaking out. She's definitely hating on me."

Shannon twisted her fingers. "I'll fix it! I'll—"

"Go home, Shan," I said. "That's the best thing you can do. Please. Just go."

"But...but that's exactly what I don't want to do! I'll lose you..." she trailed off, her throat working as she glanced away.

I placed my hands on her shoulders and squeezed them. "You *divorced* me. You lost me then."

She flinched.

"You didn't want what I did. Remember what you told me? Genuine love doesn't keep people from their dreams, the life they want to live. I want to live my life with Keelie. She's my future, Shan. We're...we're just memories."

Tears spilled over Shannon's lashes and down her cheeks as her lip quivered. As always, her tears wrenched something inside me.

Keelie didn't cry often. She bottled her emotions up tight, but that fracturing of her eyes, the look of betrayal that settled over her face cracked my ribs wide and flailed my heart much more than these tears. The hurt I'd caused Keelie cut deep because it was so unexpected.

I would always regret that she'd seen Shannon's attempt to renew our former life together. Because Keelie had jumped to the obvious conclusion—and the wrong one.

More tears spilled over Shannon's lashes, but she nodded. "I'm losing you all over again."

"That's because I'm ready to live again. Fully. With a woman I love… Look, I don't want to hurt you, but Keelie is everything to me. The problem is, she didn't have an easy time growing up, and she's always expecting us to fall apart. Now I need to focus on getting her back."

Shannon narrowed her eyes, her mind already churning. "What problems?"

I shook my head. "That's her story, not mine. And it's none of your business."

"But you're going to marry her, have kids with her? If she's messed up, will this be a stable environment for your kids?"

"Stop trying to manipulate me," I said, voice soft. "You're better than that."

She pressed her lips together and nodded, once. "I should be." She sucked in a ragged breath as she rose from the step. "So this is goodbye?"

I nodded. "You were the most important person in my life."

"You're still that to me."

I shook my head. "No, I'm not. And we both know it. I haven't been for a long time."

She nodded once more, then turned on her heel and walked toward her car—a Mercedes. Shannon loved her luxury items. So unlike Keelie, who was most comfortable in Target-bought jeans and a soft, two-year-old tee. I'd fallen for two very different women, and I couldn't be happier with my second choice.

I inhaled long and slow as I accepted what Shannon had somehow known back then—we'd never have made it long-term. That didn't diminish what she'd once been to me, but my time with her was passed. Long since.

Maxim sped into my driveway just as Shannon pulled out.

"What's going on?" he asked.

"Keelie walked in right when Shannon tried to put the moves on me."

Maxim's eyes widened. "That's not good."

"No, and we have to be at the airport in an hour and a half, so I don't have time to go by her place." I kicked his tire as I let loose a stream of curses.

"Creative but not helpful. Get your bag. I'll drive while we strategize."

Houston traffic remained heavy and unpredictable, so my initial plan to find Keelie and explain fizzled. I couldn't *not* go, either. She expected the worst from everyone. I couldn't be that man. I refused to be that man.

But, as Maxim pointed out, I couldn't let my teammates

down, and if I wasn't on the plane, Coach wouldn't let me play. These next two games would seal our seed spot, and our stats showed how much better the team was when I was on the ice. Leaving rookie Luka there to get hammered on the boards wasn't an option.

For the first time in my life, I cursed my responsibilities to my team. Mainly because I longed to put Keelie first. Where she belonged.

If she'd let me. If she could see past her hurt and realize I wasn't her father.

CHAPTER 52
Keelie

Tears blurred my vision too much to continue driving. I pulled over and leaned my head on my arms. The sobs shook my body, causing everything to ache.

Damn Cormac for his lies. If he'd been honest about his relationship with his ex—that he was using me to get her back, I guess—I would have made different choices. As in, I never would have let him into my life. Into my heart.

Seeing Cormac embracing Shannon gutted me. I'd watched my future spin out into a hazy, scary blackness I couldn't control.

I rested my cheek on the steering wheel, enjoying the coolness against my overheated cheeks. I tucked my hair behind my ears and took a deep breath. My phone rang with Ida Jane's ringtone. I snatched it up and answered. "If Cormac asked you to talk to me, I'm hanging up."

"Where are you?" Ida Jane asked.

"I don't know." Listlessly, I looked around. "I'm going to my house, I guess."

"I'll meet you there," Ida Jane said.

"Don't bother," I said, tears clogging my throat. Good thing I'd never mentioned my plan to sell my house. I wouldn't move—especially not in with Cormac.

I'd spent my entire life unloved.

I refused to submit to such a life in the future.

CHAPTER 53
Cormac

Clenching my jaw, I stared up at the flag, trying to get my head in the game. If we beat the Predators, we'd play Montreal in the first round of the playoffs.

I wanted a rematch against Dukovsky, and I planned to win again. While I was quite pleased he hadn't taken the Cup *and* my ex-wife back in the day, I didn't feel as if I'd earned that championship. I hadn't suited up after game five, and my old team had ground out a win in game seven.

But this time, I was captain. I was the veteran the others turned to. So when the puck dropped, I was ready. Nik won the drop and shot the puck toward me. I skated hard around Evanovich, who tried to high-stick me.

The whistle stopped play, and we all groaned. Damn, we needed some momentum.

My chance came midway through the second period when Maxim slid me a sweet little wrist-flick. I tapped the puck down, moving my stick to keep Evanovich off the prize, and skated around the back of the net. Their goalie sank low, so I shot high and hard—right over his helmet into the back of the net! I lifted my arms, cheering. And Evanovich slammed me into the boards.

I grunted. He was pushing the boundaries, ready for a fight.

"Ignore him," Nik said, patting my back.

"Hell of a shot," Maxim yelled.

Adam nodded from our goal, his grin obvious even through the mesh of his mask.

"First blood of the playoffs!" Cruz hooted.

Nashville pushed back hard, but Adam blocked their two attempts on goal, and then Nik managed a second goal.

Just like he had with me, Evanovich came in low and hard, slamming him into the boards. Nik grimaced, grabbing his ribs, but the refs were already there, pushing the players apart.

"He needs to be dealt with," I snarled as I came over the boards for a rest. The frustration and anger in the game mirrored my inability to sort out the situation with Keelie. I hated feeling impotent.

That's why I lured Evanovich into another dirty hit. Even before the shock of his mass slamming me into the boards reverberated, I'd pulled off my gloves. I enjoyed slamming my fist into his cheek…maybe a little too much.

Unlike the last time I got into an altercation, this time my team thumped my shoulders and back. Not gonna lie—felt good to know they were proud of me.

I was proud, too. A pool of water formed under my skates and between my legs as I sucked in a breath. I'd missed a crucial fourteen minutes of the game, but the boys held on, fighting Nashville off and finishing with the win.

Coach Whittaker beckoned me toward the small office off the visitor's locker room. I strode in, wincing. I should have unlaced my skates, but I'd been too nervous…and too superstitious to change anything until I heard that final buzzer.

Silas Whittaker, a former forward like me, stood with his back straight and thick chest out. The guy was pushing forty, and a few gray hairs swirled through the brown, but he still looked like one of the boys. He'd proven to be a hell of a good coach, able to listen, cajole, and tease out the best in his players. He'd traded just two guys—and the rest of us had cheered their removal. Coach was fair but tough—my favorite type of leader.

He tapped his new glasses on the folded paper that lay on the desk. He kept his attention on me as he lowered into the chair. He motioned for me to sit, so I did. His brows tugged in tight over his nose, causing a ripple of wrinkled skin to flow up his forehead. "I heard about your off-ice drama," he began.

A pang hit my guts, but I sat up straighter. "From Paloma?"

"Yeah, she was with Naomi and Nicole when Maxim's girl-friend called."

I was glad our CATS were so tight-knit. Keelie needed her friends to help her through her hurt since she wouldn't talk to me.

I nodded. "It's been a rough couple of days, even with that all-important W in our column."

"I almost didn't sign the trade for you from Montreal," Coach said.

My stomach dropped as his words settled around me.

"You were angry, out of control, unwilling to talk to anyone or work out your feelings anywhere other than the ice. You had the highest minutes in the PB of any player that season. Still one of the highest in the sport."

I folded my fingers around my knees and focused on taking in a deep breath, letting it out. Coach slid on his glasses as he picked up a paper. He read for a second, then set it aside.

"Evonavich hit Sidorov late. We're lucky he didn't break something with that check to the knees. It was dirty. You skating to the ref and complaining forced the review. I get why you threw down with Evonavich after he checked you, too—that fucker needs to learn a lesson, and sending him sprawling and bloody did that for our boys and the rest of the league. By the way, Stol was out for blood. If he'd gone over the boards, he would have pounded Evonavich."

I held my breath, unsure what Coach was telling me.

"You waited, let Evonavich come at you first…that meant control. So have the calls from other players to the commissioner. From what he's said, most have praised your actions."

Coach slid his glasses from his nose and stared down at me. "I've watched you struggle with your personal life, unable to leave it off the ice. That's your greatest weakness as a player. That's why I worried about taking you on, no matter how stellar your stats were—outside of the penalty minutes." He smirked, but I remained stone-faced.

Was he planning to trade me? My heart pounded hard against my ribs as sweat slicked my sides. I needed to be in Houston, near Keelie. I loved the life I'd built there, and I didn't want to restart again.

My gaze snapped back to Coach Whittaker's as he continued. "But you handled it. You worked through your business, and you kept your cool. The ejection for the game is the totality of your punishment, and even better, Evonavich is out for three games.

You were a leader, both on the ice and off. Which makes me even happier that I looked beyond your lippy orneriness all those years ago and saw the man you could be. The man you've become."

My Adam's apple bobbed as I struggled to process Coach's comments. So…he *wasn't* trading me?

"Now, get the hell out of this office and sort out your personal life."

I rose on shaky legs, dipping my head. This meeting hadn't gone the way I'd expected. Joy blossomed in my chest. Coach considered me a genuine leader of the team—a man the younger guys should look up to. A man worthy of offering guidance.

He was a father figure even though he had less than a decade on me.

"Thanks, Coach," I said, my voice raspy with emotion. "I'll do my best to make sure you don't have reason to doubt me."

"See that you do, Bouchard. For the record, I like your lady. She's a damn fine golfer and the exact kind of woman we need leading our CATS."

Pride intermingled with concern. "We'll see if I can convince her to hear me out."

Coach rose from the chair and snagged his clipboard as he rounded the desk.

"You're a stubborn cuss. I'd put my money on you." He slapped my shoulder and strode out.

CHAPTER 54
Keelie

The knocking on my door refused to stop. I checked the peep-hole and gasped, shoving the back of my hand against my lips. Shannon, the love of Cormac's life, stood at my door. She wore the same outfit I'd admired when I'd walked in on them getting cozy earlier. It was a silky sheath dress with an embroidered bolero jacket and nude heels. Her hair was tucked back in a neat chignon at the base of her neck. Pearls encircled her slim throat.

I chewed hard on my lower lip, taking in my worn jeans. I'd dressed for comfort in the sneakers with the arch support that I wore most days, thanks to the hours on my feet. My shirt was one of my nicer ones, but that wasn't saying much. It was a button-up blouse I'd purchased from an online thrift shop, already secondhand. But I'd liked the fluted neck and the slim cut that I thought accentuated my figure.

"Keelie?" she called.

I jerked, barely keeping myself from banging against the wall. My heart fluttered. I couldn't talk to this woman—we weren't in the same league. No wonder Cormac wanted her.

"I know you're home. I heard you… Look, I just want to talk. I need to explain what you walked in on earlier. Please let me in. *Please*, Keelie. Mac doesn't deserve to be punished for my mistakes."

I shoved my palms against my aching stomach, unsure how to handle this newest hell of a situation.

"Let her in," Ida Jane hissed from the kitchen.

I scowled at her, but she scowled back with just as much ferocity.

"He loves you, Keelie," Shannon said. "He told me so right after he asked me to go home."

Before I realized I'd done it, I opened the door even as I glowered at the taller, glamorous woman. I was above-average height, but Shannon Lavoie Bouchard had three inches on me at least—more in her heels.

"Then why are you here?" I asked.

"Because I couldn't leave knowing I was the reason for the mess between the two of you." She sighed, her eyes glistening with tears. "I've always loved Mac, and I always will. He was a wonderful boy who turned into a magnificent man."

Hot jealousy slid its sharp edge through my chest and into my belly. She had so much history with him. How could I ever compete?

I started to shut the door, but she gripped the frame, her slim fingers turning white. Shannon wasn't in control of her emotions. Her eyes were red-rimmed, and her cheeks blotchy.

She cleared her throat. "Cormac was always going to shine. *Always.* If I wasn't careful, I'd be left in his shadow. I made it into a competition he didn't know we were having. He wanted kids, but I postponed, put him off because I knew if I became a mother, I'd have to give up what I'd created for myself. So I pushed him away, divorced him in order to give myself space to come into my own.

But now…" She swallowed. "He's moved on."

She said this as if it were a shock of unimaginable proportions. Part of me wanted to know what man would turn his back on Shannon, too, but a much larger part of me rallied around Cormac. She'd hurt him, thrown him away—embarrassed him. And she'd expected him to wait until she was ready for more. My hands clenched. Him getting serious about me appeared to have been that catalyst. I studied her…and saw anger that I'd taken her favorite toy.

"You always planned to take him back," I said, "like he was a dog on a long leash."

My anger caused her to flinch, her throat working as she struggled for control. Her lips trembled as she failed.

Oh, hell. She wasn't evil; she was self-absorbed. And right now, her world lay shattered around her. My empathy kicked in hard, just like it did with my students. I opened the door further and took her arm, leading her to the armchair in my small living room. I plopped back down on the hand-me-down couch and offered her a tissue from the box on the coffee table.

"If you love him, and you still want him, why are you willing to give him up?" Her showing up, telling me this didn't make sense.

She sniffled, dabbing at her eyes. "Because I don't want kids more than I do want Mac," she said.

My hand fell to my stomach, fingers curling protectively around the nonexistent bump.

She offered a wan smile as her gaze rose from my palmed belly to my face. "I see you don't have that issue."

I shook my head. We stared at each other. "May I ask…*why*?" I asked.

She shrugged and sighed. "Who knows? I just don't. At all. The idea…" She shuddered. "We tried for a while, a few months before I served him papers."

I worked hard not to flinch at the idea of Cormac and Shannon together like that. I wanted to rip her eyes out and scream, vanquishing my foe. But—*wow*, I was bloodthirsty. How shocking. I clasped my hands together to keep from lashing out.

"When I realized he was serious about you, I couldn't stand it." She ripped the tissue. "His mother made it seem like he was just angry, getting even with me, that all I had to do was show him I wanted him back. So I concocted this plan where I'd give him a child—*one*—and I could continue to live my life, but with him as my husband. I had it all planned out." Her laugh was watery, filled with recrimination. "I never asked him if that's something *he* wanted. I just blew into his place and started talking. I was wrong. I didn't respect him or you, what you two have built these past few months. And what you saw was my attempt to take him back to a place that wasn't healthy, all because I don't want to lose him." More tears streamed down her cheeks. "He loves you. His first action was to go after you."

I slid my hands down my front all the way to my knees, my mind whirring. "I don't know what to say."

She rose. "There's nothing for you to say. Just…be better to him than I was."

She strode to the door and out, clicking it shut behind her.
Ida Jane, Naomi, and Nicole spilled from my kitchen.

"That's the most selfless act I've ever seen," Nicole whispered.

"Pfft. Only because it followed years of selfish ones," Naomi said. She bee-lined back to the kitchen and pulled out the pints of ice cream she'd brought over a little while ago. Grabbing spoons, she handed me the carton of double chocolate fudge brownie before popping the top off her caramel swirl. She dug in.

"I was really enjoying my full-on hate of her," Naomi muttered.

"You can keep that," Ida Jane said, pointing her spoon at Naomi. "She arrived in town prepared to break up Cormac and Keelie."

"Good point," Nicole said, shoveling a bite into her mouth. "This is good."

I scowled down into my creamy chocolate goodness. I put a spoonful into my mouth, but the ice cream didn't soothe my aching belly. "I should have let him explain."

"Yes, you should have," Ida Jane said. She'd been on Team Cormac all day.

I scowled at her.

"Shhhh! She's having a breakthrough," Naomi said.

"She needs to hurry up so I can stop eating ice cream. This shit makes me bloat, but dammit, it tastes so good. I *really* need to move into happy-dance mode," Nicole mumbled.

"Are we going to watch the game?" Ida Jane asked.

"Shhh!" Nicole said.

"I'm turning it on. I can't miss Adam's game," Naomi said.

Cormac had never given me a reason, not a hint, that he even glanced at other women until yesterday. My insecurities, thanks to my father, were as much to blame as Shannon's continued love for a wonderful man.

I burst into tears.

"Oh, oh. Why are you crying?" Ida Jane sounded panicked. "Um, Kee, stop crying b-because if you d-don't, I-I'm going to start... Shit!"

Ida Jane burst into noisy tears, dropping her forehead to my shoulder. We sobbed and heaved until I was spent. Ida Jane took another moment to calm down. She took the tissue I offered her, and we both mopped our faces.

With a huff, she picked up her carton again and licked the melting concoction from the spoon. "You have to be my BFF for life now that you made me snot on you," she said.

"Of course." I nodded. "You already were, anyway." I wrapped my arm around her shoulder. "You're the best bestie."

"We're *all* BFFs," Naomi snapped. "Now eat your ice cream. We need sustenance if we're going to watch the game on this tiny TV."

I picked up my carton and tried another spoonful of the melted, creamy goodness. This time, my stomach felt a little better.

CHAPTER 55
Keelie

"Why did I let you talk me into this?" I muttered as we walked down the long hallway toward the locker room.

Naomi slurped her soda, unperturbed by my growing dismay. "One, you look super cute. Two, you're bad at relationships and wanted my advice, which I gave you. Three, you realized your guy is super fucking amazing, and you wanted to dish a bit of that love back."

The temporary tattoo stretched on my cheek as I scowled. I eased my face back into neutral lines. "I feel ridiculous."

"And you might look ridiculous, too, but what's more important? Your pride or your love for your guy?" Ida Jane piped in from my other side.

The only one of our crew missing was Nicole, and that was only because she had to parent her kids. Naomi, Ida Jane, and I had road-tripped up to Dallas this morning. And now that I was here, I was panicking.

I crossed my hands over my belly, giving it a surreptitious rub. "You don't have to talk so much sense. It's irritating."

Naomi raised a brow as she took another long pull of her soda. I laughed as I turned away.

Now that Ida Jane and Naomi were in my life, I'd realized the wrongness of my relationship with Marian—namely that it had never been a real relationship, which wasn't that different from the problems with my previous attempts at romance.

I gave, and others took from me. Only now had I found people who supported me, who loved me enough to give back to me—to want my happiness as much as, and maybe more than, their own. Adjusting to that reality would take time, and I wasn't completely there. But I was on my way.

Once Cormac and I talked...

As we approached the locker room, there were a few people milling around. Two of them kept shouting questions.

"Reporters," Naomi muttered. "Ignore them."

CHAPTER 56
Cormac

A full twenty-four hours after the terrible incident, I still didn't know where my relationship stood with Keelie, and that unknown ate at me. I'd slept poorly. My usual aches from getting and throwing hits at opponents were amplified, and I groaned.

"What's wrong?" Nik asked, peering up from lacing his skate.

He had some complicated practice that required starting from scratch each time. Growing a beard, wearing the same socks, undershirt, or even lucky underwear—washed, because otherwise athlete's foot would eat the skin—I could understand. But a ritual that required re-lacing a skate, and measuring the length after each loop, was too strange for me to grasp.

"Lace up," I said. "We have a game to win."

"Hell yeah!" Cruz bellowed. But once he got a good look at my face, his happy expression—which meant he looked like a crazed serial killer—disappeared. He now seemed more like an angry bear, a much better look for him. It fit with the bushy facial hair and wild mane that exploded from the bottom of his helmet.

"She didn't call you?" he asked.

I shook my head.

"But…"

Coach strolled in, his assistants fanning out behind him. I smiled at this display because Silas Whittaker wasn't big on the power trip. Still, he needed a staff to fill the gaps he couldn't attend to in real-time. Houston's team wasn't flashy, but we were a cohesive bunch, and that started with the man who now tugged his glasses up on top of his head with a grimace of annoyance.

"All right, settle down." He waited, but not long. Even Luka, the rowdy rookie, turned his face toward Coach, expression expectant.

"Last night, you played well—like a team." He met each player's gaze. "I want more of that tonight because that's how we'll win the Stanley Cup next month. Sure, stats pad your personal résumé, but by playing smarter, by playing together as a unit, we break through their defense. Did you know that chimps hunt in packs? They have blockers, a decoy, and a hunter. By all sticking to their roles, they're successful eighty percent of the time."

"I didn't know chimps ate meat," Cruz muttered.

"Now you do," Coach said, pointing at him. "I watched the show with Trix. So, tonight, we go out there and fight."

"Guess it's time to be a chimp," Cruz added, put off by the analogy.

"Better than a bonobo," Adam said, coming over to wrap his arms around one of Cruz's shoulders and one of mine. "They're peaceful. We don't need a kumbaya circle. We need to kick ass, and chimpanzees are vicious little fucks."

"I thought that was gorillas," Nik said, frowning.

"Nah, man, they like to enjoy their ladies and sleep," Adam clarified. "It's the chimps you got to worry about." At our looks, he shrugged. "I watched that documentary, too. It was interesting."

He dropped his arm from Cruz's shoulder and swung toward

me, putting both hands on my shoulders. "Your girl's outside the locker room."

"What?"

"I'm sure it's supposed to be some big surprise-reveal bull-shit—like those dumb gender parties for babies where people burn down forests."

"That shit's weird. As weird as comparing us to a chimp hunt," Cruz said, shaking his head.

Adam grinned. "Be sure to tell her she looks cute in her Wild-catters gear."

I groaned. Like Adam, I loved seeing my girl in my sweater. There was something so primal, so right about it.

He leaned in closer. "And it's a good thing this game starts late and we're staying in Dallas tonight." He winked before he walked back to his locker to grab his goalie mask.

Coach smiled. "You can have five minutes in the team office."

Joy blasted through the hard knot in my belly, pressing outward, easing the bruises covering my body. "Thanks."

"Be a chimp!" Cruz bellowed.

"You idiot! Mac needs to be one of those bonobos," Adam said.

"Nah, a gorilla," Maxim said. "You said they were good with the ladies, remember?"

I pushed through, and then the heavy metal doors slid shut behind me, shutting off their argument.

Keelie stood there like a rabbit caught in headlights. She tilted her head back as my palm slid along the back of her neck, and I kissed her. She gripped my arms and kissed me back. When we pulled apart, I rested my forehead against hers.

"I've been worried," she breathed. "And upset."

I lifted my head, scowling at the cameras turned in our direction. I tugged her toward the door. "Coach said we have five minutes."

CHAPTER 57
Cormac

Keelie trailed behind me as I clomped into the small space. She turned to face me before I shut the door. "I was wrong to run off. You've never done anything, not once, to make me question you. I let my past nearly take my future from me. From *us*."

Her jaw trembled, so I cupped it. "I'll always be there for you, pretty girl. Just you. We're together. A team."

She rose up on her toes, and I dropped down so we could kiss again.

"I'm selling my house and moving in with you."

I smiled. "Or you can rent it out and have another income stream. But yes, I want you with me. *Always*." I leaned in closer and ran my nose along her cheek. "I asked Ida Jane to go ring shopping with me next Friday."

She gasped. "That little sneak! She didn't say anything."

Voices jostled outside the door. I was pretty sure the guys were crowded around it—so much for them pretending they were above emotions. They'd been all up in my business from the moment I got involved with Keelie.

"I can't hear!"

I rolled my eyes and shook my head. That was Cruz. He hated being left out of anything.

"Because I swore her to secrecy," I told Keelie.

She pursed her lips. "I guess that explains why she was so sure I'd misinterpreted the scene between you and Shannon."

More grumblings outside the door. My guess was the guys were jockeying for position. When the door squeaked open, I shot a scowl toward the huddled mass of players. Nik waved back before the door closed again.

"Shannon's a memory. You, though, you're my future."

Keelie blinked up at me. I loved her sky-blue eyes and dark-honey hair. "Will you ask me...now?"

"Is that what you want?"

She smiled. "Yes."

I dropped to one knee with an awkward grunt. Kneeling in skates wasn't the easiest action. "Keelie Marie Hayes, will you make me the happiest man ever and marry me?"

"Say yes!" Maxim called as the door opened again. He leaned over Naese, trying to get a better view of us in the small room.

"You just want to use her agreement as leverage for Ida Jane," Adam shot back.

"So?" Maxim asked.

"This is much better than chimpanzee wars," Cruz said.

"He needs something to put on her finger," Nik said.

"We really need to win this hockey game now," Stol said. "Fuck, if we don't, Mac's marriage won't make it."

"Don't go ruining it before it's even started. Shit, man," Naese said.

"Here, we made you a ring," Maxim said. He shoved it into my hand. It was a twisted mess of gum wrappers.

I raised it up, and the guys cheered.

Keelie threw her head back and laughed from her belly as I tugged her onto my thigh. "Y-yes," she gasped through her giggles. "Always." She sobered as I slipped the weird ring on her finger. She clasped my cheeks. "You're mine, Cormac Bouchard."

I kissed her again. "I've been telling you that for months."

EPILOGUE
Cormac

"I'm sorry you didn't win the Cup." Keelie settled in my lap, her arms around my neck. Her tiny bikini barely covered her luscious tits. I skated my hand up her side and settled it over one. There was something about a beach wedding…

We were on Kauai at a posh resort. Keelie and I had rented a private bungalow out over the water, and we were in our bedroom. Filmy white drapes fluttered in the windows, and the soft sounds of rippling water drifted in. I lay on the bed, leaning against the thick teak headboard, with Keelie in my lap. She'd wanted to go for a night swim. I'd tugged her over here.

"That's okay. We pushed all the way to the last game. Other teams know we're contenders."

"Taking out Dukovsky in the first round helped a lot with your attitude."

I grinned. "I still hate that fucker."

Keelie giggled. "He's not looking so hot with his suspension going into next year."

"Or the problem with his knee."

Keelie gasped. "Really? That's too bad. Do you think he'll retire?"

"Don't care." I pressed my erection against her hip. "I have much better things to think about. And feast on." I waggled my brows. "Come closer…"

When she did, I kissed her, loving how she tasted. My hand drifted down to her still-flat stomach, and I palmed her belly, rubbing my fingertips back and forth.

"How's my peanut?"

"Peachy," Keelie replied. "But his or her mama's frustrated that you knocked her up just before the wedding." She pouted, but there was no heat behind her words. In fact, her smile grew so wide, I couldn't help but match it. "No fun drinks for me this trip."

"But wonderful memories. Fantastic ones we'll treasure." I didn't bother to reiterate that I was with her, one hundred percent, through this pregnancy. She knew how much this child meant to me—how much *she* meant. I untied her top and threw it aside. I pinched her nipples, eliciting a gasp.

"Sensitive," she said.

I smiled as I nuzzled her breasts.

"This is the last time I get to love you as Keelie Hayes."

"Mmm… I'm looking forward to being Keelie Bouchard," she said.

"Not as much as I am." I untied the strings to her bottoms and tossed them aside, too.

I shimmied out of my swim trunks just as she sank down on my dick.

"You feel so good." She rode me at her own pace, bringing us both to rippling satisfaction.

I gripped her hand, loving my engagement ring on her finger. Tomorrow, I'd add another ring in front of my hockey family and our friends. Neither Keelie's parents nor mine were invited, but that was okay.

We'd made our own family, one built on a foundation of love and respect.

The next day, we said our vows in the bright Hawaiian sunshine. Keelie wore a beautiful silk dress trimmed with lace and glittering beads. Coach walked her down the aisle.

And when the officiant told me I could kiss the bride, I did, with a flourish. Then, I dropped to my knees and kissed my baby.

Keelie laughed, even as tears of joy brimmed in her eyes.

That photo sat on my bedside table every day for the rest of my life.

The End

ACKNOWLEDGEMENTS

Thank you, Jessica Royer Ocken, for your expertise and your joy of the written word. It's an absolute pleasure to work with you, and I know my book is better thanks to your keen insights and sharp eyes.

Kate, thank you, thank you, thank you for the amazing beta read! This book is stronger thanks to your comments.

Thanks Charity Chimni for your time and amazing proof-reading skills. I can't tell you how much it means to have you and Mantha in my corner, cheering me on. I'm so thankful to have you on my team!

Thank you, Chris, for the gorgeous cover! I luuurrrvvvv it!!!

My lovely readers: well, clearly, without you, none of this would be possible. The fact that you trust me with your time is the greatest compliment. Thank you so, so much.

www.ingramcontent.com/pod-product-compliance
Lightning Source LLC
Chambersburg PA
CBHW070637260626
47161CB00007B/2733